Black and Blue
in the Lilac City

a collection of
509 Crime Stories

by Colin Conway

Table of Contents

What is the 509?

Separated by the Cascade Range, Washington State is divided into two distinctly different climates and cultures.

The western side of the Cascades is home to Seattle, its 34 inches of annual rainfall, and the incredibly weird and smelly Gum Wall. Most of the state's wealth and political power are concentrated in and around this enormous city. The residents of this area know the prosperity that has come from being the home of Microsoft, Amazon, Boeing, and Starbucks.

To the east of the Cascade Mountains lies nearly two-thirds of the entire state, a lot of which is used for agriculture. Washington State leads the nation in producing apples, it is the second-largest potato grower, and it's the fourth for providing wheat.

This eastern part of the state can enjoy more than 170 days of sunshine each year, which is important when there are more than 200 lakes nearby. However, the beautiful summers are offset by harsh winters, with average snowfall reaching 47 inches and the average high hovering around 37°.

While five telephone area codes provide service to the westside, only 509 covers everything east of the Cascades, a staggering twenty-one counties.

Of these, Spokane County is the largest with an estimated population of 506,000.

Foreword

At midnight on September 17, 1991, legendary hard rock band Guns N' Roses released two albums simultaneously—*Use Your Illusion I & II*. The first album featured sixteen songs, while the second carried fourteen. Both albums went onto be certified platinum many times over, and each spawned several hits.

That day was one when I immediately hauled my butt to the local record store as an album hit the shelves. Not only was GNR huge at the time, but their song "You Could Be Mine" was part of the soundtrack for *Terminator 2: Judgment Day*—the biggest movie in the world. If you've read any of my novels (and let's be honest, you should have by now), you will know I'm a fan of hard rock. Buying those two albums was a moment that still resonates in my memory.

So, why am I mentioning a legendary rock act and their multiplatinum-selling albums in this introduction? It's funny you should ask.

When I decided I wanted to release a collection of short stories based in my world of the 509 Crime Stories, I knew they would fall into two sets. The second volume—*Black and Blue in the Lilac City*—is what you hold in your hands now. I'm hoping you'll read the companion piece—*Murder by Any Other Name*. Trust me—you'll dig it. I'll wait for you if you want to buy it now...

I waffled back and forth on how to release the collections. Traditional publishers release books annually. Screw that, I thought.

Actually, I thought something more inappropriate, but I've never seen anyone swear in an introduction before, and I don't want to break with proper etiquette. So, I thought, screw that.

Publishing at a quicker pace is one of the allures of being an independent author/publisher—I can do things my way. So, what would be a reasonable period between the release of Volume I and II?

Three months? I could release them ninety days apart, but why pick that period of time? Would that make any difference? Most readers who finish a book want to move on to the next in the series. Would that be the same for a collection of short stories? I didn't have any data to work with, so I had to go with my gut. Ninety days seemed too long.

Okay, how about one month? I did that with my Cozy Up series and experienced some success. I could replicate that process again without much trouble. But why do the same thing? Why not try something new?

Releasing the collections a week apart seemed doable. It would be a ton of work only to have them separated by seven days. If I was going to release them that close together, I should go ahead and do them both on the same day. That idea seemed crazy, egotistical, and totally wrong.

Then I remembered *Use Your Illusion* and thought, "That's so rock & roll."

Again, to be truthful, I thought something improper, but as I said before, I'd never seen anyone ever swear in an introduction before. I really wanted to here, but proper etiquette is essential in situations like this.

***

So, you hold in your hands Volume II of the 509 Crime *Short* Stories. These tales are full of thieves, pimps, prostitutes, killers, and good people pushed beyond their normal limits.

You won't find serial killers in this collection. I hate them. In the world of fiction and movies, serial killers are so mind-numbingly dull and overplayed.

Many of the stories in this volume tie directly into the existing 509 world. For those of you new to the game, the novels so far are *The Side Hustle*, *The Long Cold Winter*, *The Blind Trust*, *The Suit*, *The Value in Our Lies*, and *The Mean Street*.

The story, "Remember the Rifleman," has an appearance by Jim Morgan, the detective from *The Blind Trust* and *The Value in Our Lies*.

Three of the short stories introduce characters for the sixth book in the series—*The Mean Street*. Those stories are "Daddy's Girl," "Dwight's Girl," and "Marlene."

"Foolproof" and "Price to Pay" provide a glimpse into the Hope Apartments. This place of heartbreak and desperation has its own anthology treatment as contributing authors take a tour through the world of the 509 in *The Eviction of Hope*.

The tale, "Death at Sunrise," features Major Crimes Detective Shane McAfee of the Spokane County Sheriff's Office. McAfee returns in the first installment of an amateur sleuth series that runs parallel to the 509 Crime Stories—*Strait Over Tackle*.

Some stories have no direct tie to the novels beyond the fact that they occur in the diverse world of the 509. They're included to add color to the world.

Enough talk. Let's get to the mayhem.

Colin Conway
Summer 2021

Black and Blue
in the Lilac City

Carter's View

The hammer landed on his thumb.

Dropping the tool to hold his injured hand, Carter Murphy yelped and jumped to his feet. He silently reminded himself not to curse. Instead, he ground his teeth together and forced his anger down. During their thirty-seven years of marriage, Miriam had fought against his swearing. Carter often delighted in using inappropriate language to rile her up. Now that she was gone, he rarely used the words she had disliked.

He inspected his thumb. There was no visible damage, but it throbbed like hell. He wrapped his right hand around the sore digit, closed his eyes, and emitted a low moan.

As the pain lessened, Carter reopened his eyes and looked around his neighborhood. The view from his roof provided a perspective he wasn't used to seeing.

Two houses down, Joe Critchlow's backyard was almost entirely dirt—no doubt a result of his two Great Danes. It was in stark contrast to Joe's beautifully maintained front yard. Carter couldn't understand how the man tolerated the miserable beasts, especially when they did that type of damage to his yard.

Phyllis Mitchell, now in her mid-eighties, lived next door. She stood near the flowers that ran along her rear fence line. Her husband died last year, a month before his ninetieth birthday. She was next to a sundial urn, where her husband's ashes now resided. Carter watched Phyllis whisper to the sundial for a couple of moments before he turned away, ashamed of intruding on the private moment.

Directly behind his house, a woman sunbathed. Her body glistened either from lotion or sweat caused by the late August sun. Her figure appeared trim in the small white bikini. It was the first time Carter had seen the woman. The fence between their backyards was six feet in height, with barely a crack between the boards. Perhaps she had sunbathed in her yard before, and he wouldn't have noticed it from ground level.

Carter's gaze never left the woman as he wiped his forehead with the back of his hand.

The sunlight danced on the woman's belly the way light bounces off diamonds. Even from this distance, he noticed the soft rise and fall in her stomach as she breathed. It was rhythmic, as if she were asleep. It was a beautiful day for lounging—

Suddenly, the woman sat upright and whipped off her sunglasses. With her other hand, she blocked the sun to get a better look at Carter.

This surprised him, and without hesitation or thought, he stepped backward. Forgetting he was on the roof and not a flat surface, Carter tilted severely. He took a quick step and swayed wildly for a moment. His arms flailed as he fought to recover his balance. Swinging his hand further hurt his thumb, and he pulled it into his chest.

Luckily, Carter recovered his footing. Before anything unfortunate happened, he mused.

He was not secured to the roof in a safe and approved manner that a government agency would require of a professional roofer. When he started this home improvement project, Carter considered the precautions too silly and protective, yet another overreach by the nanny state. Now, though, he thought perhaps he'd been too cavalier with that attitude.

Carter turned his attention back to the woman, who seemed to watch him with intense curiosity. He stood frozen with embarrassment. He checked his other neighbors to see if they had noticed his near fall.

None of them had.

The woman in the bikini now stood slowly to reveal herself. She extended her arms and slowly turned—a private pirouette. When she stopped spinning, she waved.

Not knowing how to handle the awkwardness of having been caught observing a nearly naked woman in her backyard, Carter did the only thing he could think of—he waved back.

The sudden hand motion renewed the pain in his thumb, and he protectively jerked it to his chest. Carter took another step backward on the slanted roof. His running shoe slipped on some shingles, and he fell.

Carter tumbled from the upper roof to land on a lower flat roof of a connected shed. This narrowly avoided a crash onto the concrete driveway below. Carter lay there with the wind knocked out of him, desperately sucking for air. Panic rushed through him as he struggled for breath.

Like a fish out of water, his mouth opened and closed helplessly. When no air arrived, he rolled quickly over to his hands and knees. The movement sent waves of pain to his brain. Tears welled in his eyes as he continued drawing for breath.

It seemed like seconds with no air until suddenly— thankfully—it was there.

Fresh air filled his lungs, and Carter breathed deeply, greedily. A smile formed on his face as the overwhelming fear slowly dissipated. He stayed on his hands and knees, enjoying the simple act of taking in and expelling air. When his breathing returned to normal, the pain in his back and neck announced its presence. Carter slowly turned over to sit on the narrow roof. He rolled his head from side to side.

He knew he was hurt. Not bad enough to go to the doctor, but bad enough to stop working. Bad enough to remain still for some time. Carter examined the scrapes on his forearms. They were large and pink, and droplets of blood formed in various places. He ran his fingers through his gray hair, wincing as he did so from the pain in his back.

He lay slowly on the flat roof and patted his shirt pocket before remembering he no longer smoked. Another vice that Miriam had long struggled with him to stop. He only succeeded after she was gone.

"You okay?"

Carter painfully pushed himself back into a sitting position and looked down at the bikini-clad woman in his driveway. She stood with her feet slightly apart and her hands on her hips. She didn't seem embarrassed to be standing in their neighborhood dressed that way, let alone in front of a man she'd never met.

"I'm okay," he muttered and struggled to stand. Carter carefully shuffled to the ladder that leaned against the shed and climbed down.

"When I saw you fall," the woman said as he descended, "I freaked out."

"Just scraped up. No worries."

"What were you doing up there?"

He glanced at the nearby dumpster, which was full of worn shingles and an old roof underlayment.

The woman followed his gaze. "Stupid question. Sorry."

"It's all right. I need to get a new roof up before winter."

"You should get those scrapes cleaned out."

"Probably." He examined his forearms again.

His world suddenly tilted, and he looked into the sky. He blinked several times, fighting back a wave of nausea.

"Are you all right?"

He felt woozy, so he lowered himself to a knee. He rested an elbow on the bent leg and closed his eyes. "Must have fallen harder than I thought."

"Should I get your wife? Is she inside?"

Carter shook his head.

"Want me to call her?"

He took a deep breath and stood. "It's okay. I'm good."

"You sure?" The woman reached out and touched his shoulder.

The woman was in her late thirties, perhaps early forties, and the most attractive person he'd talked with since his wife had passed.

Full of embarrassment, Carter said, "I've got to go."

He left the woman standing in his front yard.

***

The following morning, Carter was on the roof before eight. The morning news programs claimed the temperature would top ninety-five.

Bandages covered Carter's scrapes. He had applied an ointment Miriam always insisted he use on wounds. Beyond taking ibuprofen, there was nothing he could do about the soreness in his thumb, his back, or his neck.

Around ten, the woman in the bikini walked into her backyard. This time, the swimsuit was black. She waved at Carter, and he waved back.

"Old fool," he muttered to himself.

Throughout the morning, Carter snuck repeated glances at the woman. He wasn't sure, but he thought she might have caught him watching a couple of times.

＊

The doorbell rang shortly after two. Carter had left the roof when the heat became too much. He placed his iced tea on the kitchen table next to his chicken salad sandwich.

He opened the door and saw the woman standing with a plate of cookies cradled in her hands. A silky sarong wrapped around her waist, but she still wore the black bikini top. Beads of sweat formed on her breasts. Her sunglasses perched on the top of her head. There was no embarrassment in how she dressed for the neighborhood.

"Do you like chocolate chip cookies?"

Carter stared at the plate.

"It's a simple question," she said.

"Sure."

"Sure, it's a simple question, or sure, you like chocolate chip cookies?"

"I like chocolate chip."

"Fantastic." The woman smiled broadly. "I'm Lily. My husband and I live in the house behind you. Well, you know that, don't you?"

"Yes."

"And you're Carter, right?"

"Yes." His single-word answer was as much affirmation as it was a question of how she knew his name.

"Phyllis told me."

Carter nodded. Phyllis was the local busybody. She often walked the neighborhood, chatting with anyone who would talk with her. Phyllis did that even when Bud was alive. Now that he was gone, it must have been difficult for her since she could only talk with him via the sundial in the backyard.

"Anyway," Lily said, "I made some cookies last night," she lifted the plate for emphasis, "and thought you might like some."

With hesitation, Carter accepted the plate but said nothing further.

Lily's smile slowly faded. "I guess I better be going."

"Okay."

He stood in the doorway and watched her walk away. At the sidewalk, she looked over her shoulder and smiled.

Carter stepped back into the house and shut the door.

***

Carter returned to the roof shortly after five. Even though the sun was still up, the temperature had cooled off enough for him to do some more work on the shingles.

He tried not to pay attention to her, but Lily was in her backyard reading a book. She now wore a red bikini that appeared skimpier than the black one—if that were possible. He stole repeated glances as he tried to settle that argument.

A big man in a blue suit and tie entered the backyard through the house. She didn't acknowledge his presence until he barked something. Then she jumped, closed her book, and sat upright. He walked over and repeatedly pointed his finger in a stabbing motion. While Carter couldn't hear the actual words, he understood the tone—berating. Lily was in trouble for something.

When the man finished speaking, Lily stood. She motioned as if she were talking, but Carter still couldn't hear anything. The man abruptly grabbed Lily by the arm and yanked her away from the lounge chair. He then shoved her toward the door. Lily trotted dutifully inside. The man ambled behind her, then slammed the sliding glass door shut.

Carter turned his attention back to the roof.

***

The following morning, Carter was on top of his house again, laying another row of shingles.

Next door, Phyllis Mitchell tended the flowers around her husband's urn. From the corner of his eye, Carter caught her approaching their shared fence. He carefully moved to the edge of the roof.

"Morning, Phyllis. How's Bud?"

"Quiet as ever. Did you hear the yelling last night?"

"I must have missed it. Where was it at?"

"The house back of yours." Phyllis pointed toward Lily's home. Carter glanced in that direction. Lily was not in the backyard today, and it was almost eleven.

"The police were there, too."

Carter looked at Phyllis. "How do you know that?"

"I saw the flashing lights."

"You took a walk over there, didn't you?"

Slightly embarrassed, Phyllis looked away. "I couldn't sleep."

"What was the yelling about?"

"No idea." Phyllis knocked some dirt from her gloves. "But he sounded mad. I only walked over to see what I could see."

"And what did you see?"

"Nothing much. I went home pretty quick after that."

"Huh." Carter glanced back toward Lily's.

"How's the roof coming along?"

Carter chuckled. "Slow and hot."

"You should have hired someone younger to do that."

The smile melted from Carter's face. "I can do it just fine myself."

Phyllis shrugged before walking back to Bud's urn, muttering to herself as she went.

***

Carter leaned in and pushed the little black button. He heard a soft bing-bong inside the house. A couple of moments passed before the door opened.

Lily stood before him in a short silk robe. Her golden hair was pulled back into a bun. Dark bruising was around her left eye. Her smile was weak, nothing like the smile she'd flashed him the first time they talked.

"I figured you'd want this back." Carter handed her the plate.

Her hand absently swiped over the recently washed dish. "Did you like the cookies?"

"Sure." He'd eaten only one, then tossed the rest because they made him miss his wife. "They were good."

"I'm glad you liked them."

Carter pointed at her face. "What happened to your eye?"

"I fell."

"Okay." He turned to leave.

"Carter," Lily said. "Wait."

He turned around.

"Am I beautiful? I mean, besides the eye?"

He nodded slowly and only once. Doing so twice might give her ideas he didn't want the younger woman to have.

"Do you find me desirable?"

His brow furrowed. "Excuse me?"

"Why don't you flirt with me a little?"

"It's not right."

"Just a little."

Carter swallowed. He shouldn't have brought over the plate.

"It could be our secret."

"I don't need any secrets."

"Everybody *has* secrets, Carter, but nobody *needs* them."

Had he not brought the plate, she might have come to his house. Still, this was not a good idea. He needed to leave.

"If you want—" Lily opened her robe, exposing her naked body. Several more significant bruises covered her left side. "—you can have me."

Carter glanced around the neighborhood before turning back to Lily. "Close your robe."

She kept her hands in place, not shutting the garment. "You don't like me?"

"I've got to go."

He was at the sidewalk when he heard the front door softly close.

***

Carter didn't hear her until she was at his shoulder. He'd been in the process of nailing a shingle to the roof.

She wore khaki shorts, a blue T-shirt, and white tennis shoes. Oversized sunglasses hid the bruise Carter knew was still there. "I came to help," she said.

"You should get down before you get hurt."

"Come on." Lily picked up a loose shingle. "Let me help."

"It's not a good idea." Carter rolled into a sitting position.

"Why isn't it a good idea? You're doing it alone. An extra pair of hands wouldn't hurt."

"It doesn't look good."

"Because I'm married?"

"That's one reason. Another is that I'm at least thirty years older than you."

Lily bent the pliable shingle. "If I don't care about your age, why do you care about my marital status?"

"Call me old-fashioned."

She tossed the shingle and watched it float like a frisbee into Carter's front yard.

"That wasn't nice," he said.

"What if I refuse to get off this roof?"

"Why would you do that?"

"To get my way." She put her hands on her hips and pouted.

Carter shook his head. His morning was now interrupted, and he wanted nothing more than to get this woman away from him. "Let's get off the roof."

"And do what?"

"I'll make some coffee."

"You got sugar to go with it?"

Lily went first and scampered down the ladder. As Carter prepared to leave the roof, he caught Phyllis

Mitchell watching him from her backyard. She shook her head, then hurried toward her husband's urn, no doubt anxious to share what she'd just witnessed.

***

"My husband, Bill, is already out of jail."

They were seated at Carter's kitchen table, both with a cup of coffee. Lily had already added milk and sugar to hers. She was adding another spoonful of sugar as she continued to talk.

Her statement about her husband was in response to Carter asking how the coffee was.

"One night for smacking around his wife," Carter said. "That seems fast."

"I don't know. Maybe. He's got a good attorney. A college buddy."

"What are you going to do now?"

"Me? Nothing. What would I do?"

"Leave."

Her smile was wry. "That's funny."

"He wouldn't allow it?"

She shook her head.

"If you stay, he'll do it again."

"This wasn't the first time. Won't be the last. He said it would be, but I don't believe him. He's said it before."

Carter sipped his coffee. "Where is he now?"

"The office. Always the office."

"Can I ask a question?"

"You've already asked several. What's stopping you now?"

"Why did he hit you?"

Lily shrugged, then stared into her caramel-colored coffee. "We moved in last week. Did you know that?"

"No."

"I haven't finished unpacking the boxes, and the house is still a mess. He's working, so it's my responsibility to get the house together. I played in the sun instead."

"That's not worth a beating."

"He figured it was. Me too, if I'm being honest."

"Don't you want to get away from him?"

Lily shrugged again. "I don't know. I figure I deserve it sometimes."

"No one deserves that."

A smile hinted at her lips. "That old cliché? No, I deserved it. I did before, too. For a lot worse. I've cheated on him—a couple times even."

Carter stared at her.

"Does that bother you?"

"Wasn't me you did it to."

"He knocked me around good after those times, but it was worth it." Lily stared at him, challenging him with her confession. "Go ahead and ask your question. I can see you want to ask something. It's in your eyes."

"How did he find out?"

She seemed slightly disappointed by his question. "How do you think?"

"I don't know. That's why I asked."

"How did he find out I cheated on him?" Lily ran her finger around the rim of her cup. "I told him," she said flatly.

Carter's cup of coffee hovered near his lip. He set it down without taking a sip. "Why do that?"

"They say confession is good for the soul."

"Did you know he'd hurt you?"

"Of course. I deserved it."

Carter sipped his coffee then. It was a mistake inviting this woman into his house. Nothing good could come from this moment. He was sure of it. Getting her off the roof had been necessary, but he'd made a bad situation even worse by inviting her in to have a coffee.

"Can I ask you something, Carter?"

He nodded as he held his cup with both hands—almost praying for guidance at this moment.

"Have you been with a woman since?"

"Since?"

"Since your wife passed?"

Carter put the cup down and crossed his arms over his chest. The time for prayer was over.

"Phyllis told me. Don't be mad."

"I'm not mad."

"Then tell me."

"No."

"You get what I'm asking? What I'm offering."

"Yes."

"Then why won't you tell me?"

"Because of Miriam. She wanted me to be a better man."

"Miriam? That was your wife? Phyllis didn't tell me her name. Do you think Miriam would be mad at you for moving on?"

"You're married," he said.

"You don't have to remind me."

"I think I do."

Lily dipped her spoon into the sugar again and lifted another spoonful into her cup. She swirled it around while she thought.

"You should probably go," Carter said. "I need to get back to work."

"You really want me to go?"

"It's for the best."

She let go of her spoon, and it clattered on the edge of her cup. "Have it your way, Carter, but let me tell you something—either we tumble in the hay or we don't. It's completely your call."

"We don't."

"And that's fine." Lily stood. "But I'm going to go home and tell Bill we did it, nonetheless."

He frowned. "Why would you do that?"

"Like I said, confession is good for the soul."

Carter's chest hurt. "We didn't do anything."

"But I want to. And I know you want to. I've seen the way you look at me from your roof. The bible says you shouldn't covet another man's wife. It's as bad as actually sleeping with her. You might as well give in."

"I think you'd better go."

"I'm going." Lily bent quickly and kissed his forehead. "We could have had some fun together, Carter."

He didn't watch her go.

***

That evening, a pounding on the door awoke Carter.

He climbed out of bed, pulled on a pair of pajama bottoms, but remained bare-chested. He grabbed his .45 from the nightstand and padded quickly to the front door as the pounding continued.

Carter yanked open the door and startled the big man on the other side as his left fist poised for yet another knock. The man hunched slightly and pulled his hand down. In his right hand, he held a baseball bat. His eyes flared with anger.

"You screwed my wife!"

With those four words, he immediately knew who it was—Lily's husband, Bill.

Carter gripped the gun tightly at his waist and pointed it directly at the man's belly. "You got it wrong, pal."

"Don't pal me," he shouted, then loudly inhaled through his mouth. "Lily told me what you did."

"We didn't do anything."

"She said!"

"She lied. It's time you go home."

Bill glared at the gun in Carter's fist. "You wouldn't dare."

"Don't try me."

"Lily wouldn't lie," he hollered and moved toward Carter.

***

Later the next afternoon, after the cops were gone, Carter took a shower and dressed in a pair of jeans and a T-shirt. He walked around the block, then stopped at the house he didn't want to visit. But before he could press the bell's button, she opened the door.

Her face was newly bruised, and her eyes were red, apparently from crying.

Neither one of them said anything for several seconds. They just stared at each other.

Finally, Carter said, "This… outcome. Is it what you wanted?"

When she responded, her voice was that of a small child—petulant and defiant. "Why'd you have to kill him?"

"You lied to him."

Her brow furrowed, and she thrust her lower lip out in a pout. "You didn't have to kill him."

"The police think we had a relationship, that we were intimate."

Lily wiped her eyes with the palms of her hands. "So?"

"Why would you tell them that?"

"We were just having some fun. It didn't mean anything."

Carter wondered if she was saying it had been a game that she played along with her husband. Or was she trying to say it was a game that she and Carter were playing against her husband? Either way, it turned his stomach.

"Lady, there's something seriously wrong with you."

"Me? There's something wrong with you."

"Probably."

"Not probably," Lily said. "For sure. I didn't kill my husband. That was you." She pointed at him. "You did that."

"I didn't rile the man up with lies and send him to his death."

Her lip curled in disgust. "Why are you here?" she asked. "Do you think I'll make good on my offer?"

"What?"

"Oh my God, that's what you thought, isn't it?" She laughed a single, cruel bark. "You thought if you killed my husband that we could have a relationship. I see it now."

"What?" Carter repeated.

"I was being nice, and you took it the wrong way. Probably because you were lonely after the death of your wife. Right? That's what it was."

He shook his head. "You already told the cops that we were together."

"I'll change my story. I'll tell them I was distraught and confused."

Carter held up his hands and backed away.

"You pursued me." Lily stepped onto the front porch. "I didn't want any of this to happen." She motioned between him and her. "I would never be with a man your age. You're as old as my father."

"You showed me your body."

"Were you spying on me?"

"I— What?"

"You spied on me! Didn't you? That's how you saw me naked."

Carter stepped back again. "Leave me alone."

"You started this! You caused this!"

"No. I didn't do this."

"You're lying. You spied on me from that roof of yours. Then you watched me and saw me naked." Her voice rose in hysterics. "You killed my husband! It's your fault! You got him to your house, and you ambushed him!"

Carter lifted his hands. "Listen, until I'm done with my roof, stay out of your backyard. Then I don't care what you do."

She leaned in. "I'll do what I want, where I want, and that includes going into my backyard. Got it?"

"I'm asking you—nicely."

"If you don't like it, hire someone to fix your goddamned roof. And make sure they aren't a pervert like you." She slammed the door.

Carter turned around just in time to see Phyllis Mitchell walk by. She watched him—judged him—with a disapproving shake of her head.

He knew she would hurry home now and gossip to Bud about this.

Then everyone in the neighborhood would hear about it.

Price to Pay

"Being around you people makes me feel like a genius."

Jace Wheaton looked away as Antonio continued his tirade.

"And you, you stupid pig, I told you not to spend any of your money."

Ricky's legs nervously bounced as he stared at the floor, purposefully avoiding eye contact with the bigger man. Antonio stepped across the room in two large strides and slapped Ricky on the side of the face. He fell back into his chair and covered his head with his arms.

"What part of my orders didn't you understand?"

"Leave the kid alone," Monroe said.

With a burning cigarette tucked between his lips, the older black man slouched on the wooden chair at the kitchen table. His gray hair was thinning, and his nose was flattened from years of amateur and professional fights.

Antonio spun. "What did you say?"

Monroe pulled the cigarette from his mouth and pointed the filtered end as he spoke. "Leave him alone."

"You think what he did was okay?"

"I don't think that at all."

"You running the show now?"

The older man smiled and revealed a missing tooth on the upper right side of his mouth. "I ain't interested in runnin' nothin'."

"Then why don't you shut the hell up?"

Monroe snuffed the cigarette in a nearby ashtray. Then he pushed himself upright and stood toe-to-toe with Antonio. They were the same height, but the big Latino had the older man by fifty pounds.

Antonio puffed his chest and jutted his chin out. "That's what I thought. So, why don't you keep your black—"

Monroe's gaze briefly shifted away before his fist thudded against Antonio's chin. The big Latino staggered backward before falling heavily on his ass.

Jace jumped out of his chair, upending it, and moved against the far wall. Ricky was quickly at his side.

The big man rolled over and rested his weight on one arm. He rubbed his chin with his free hand.

"You brought these boys in," Monroe said. "You knew they were young and inexperienced. It don't make no sense to beat 'em down."

Antonio glared up at the older man. "I'm never working with those two again."

"Can't say as I blame you."

"And I ain't working with you!"

Monroe shrugged. "That sounds about right." The older man thumbed toward the door. "You two better get going."

Jace turned and left. Ricky was on his heels. They ran down the hallway to the stairwell.

"What about the elevator?" Ricky asked.

Jace didn't stop to answer. If his friend was dumb enough to wait for an elevator, that was his problem. Jace was through taking chances.

At the ground floor, he shoved the stairwell door open and sprinted along the corridor toward the front entrance. One final door, and he was out in the afternoon sun. He spun around and stared at the façade of the Baker Apartments.

Next to the building's entrance, a drunk leaned against the brick wall. He opened his mouth, about to ask Jace for something, then his brow furrowed as he seemed to reconsider his question. He waved a dismissive hand and returned to murmuring to himself.

A prostitute walked up. "Wanna—"

"No."

"Asshole." She extended her middle finger.

The side door burst open, and Ricky stumbled from the building. Jace turned and walked away.

"Jace—"

He didn't stop walking.

"Jace!" Ricky hurried next to him. "Hey," he started but couldn't finish the thought. He sucked for air. Ricky reached out and grabbed Jace's arm. "Wait," he pleaded.

"No."

"Why?"

Jace jerked his arm free. "You gotta ask me why?"

Ricky bent over with his hands on his knees and greedily gulped for air.

"You screwed up, man," Jace told him.

His friend nodded, but the look in Ricky's eyes showed he had no idea how badly.

"You still don't get it."

"I'm sorry."

"What good is sorry? You weren't supposed to spend the money."

"I only wanted to impress her."

Jace tapped Ricky's temple. "Think, man. You got no job, and suddenly you buy that girl some diamond earrings. Where does she think you got the money?"

Ricky looked away.

He grabbed his friend by the front of his T-shirt, twisting it as he pulled him closer. "Did you tell her about the job? *Our* job."

"She won't rat us out."

Jace raised a hand, and Ricky flinched. Both men froze in those positions—Jace ready to strike and Ricky cowering.

A feeling of disgust rose in Jace, and he dropped his hand. "Stay away from me."

Ricky caught up to him a block away. They walked about fifty yards together before he said, "I didn't think it would hurt anything."

Jace's shoulders slumped. "That's the problem. You were too stupid to be involved in this. That's my fault."

Antonio brought Jace in. Jace brought Ricky. Actions have consequences.

They walked another block in silence. Jace crossed the street midblock, and Ricky followed. At an intersection, while they waited for traffic to thin, Ricky muttered, "They were pretty."

Jace eyed him. "Huh?"

"The earrings. They're real pretty."

"Are you kidding me?"

"No, I—"

Jace shoved Ricky into the wall of a nearby building. "Get the fuck away from me!"

Ricky didn't follow him after that.

***

It was only a few blocks to the Hope Apartments where Jace lived.

The manager's office had a windowed counter that faced into the lobby. Inside the little room, Dorothy was in an intense conversation with the maintenance man, Earl. They glanced in his direction.

"Any messages?"

Dorothy shook her head. She was in her mid-sixties and rail-thin, almost sickly so. Her face was pinched, and she fiddled anxiously with the cross she wore around her neck.

"You okay?" Jace asked.

"We aren't your answering service," Earl snapped. "You know that, right?"

Dorothy averted her gaze but still played with her silver cross. Earl jerked his head in a silent move-along gesture.

Jace's apartment was three flights up. On the door was a yellow note with big letters—NOTICE OF EVICTION. He glanced down the hallway in both directions and saw it then. Every door had the same yellow notice.

He hadn't noticed them on the way to his apartment because he was lost in his thoughts about Ricky. This must have been what Dorothy and Earl were upset about.

Jace tugged the paper from his door and read it slowly so he could understand it. Then he read it once more, just to be sure. All the residents were given one-hundred-eighty-days' notice to vacate the building.

The Hope would be redeveloped into condominiums. There'd been rumors for some time, but Jace didn't think the landlord would go through with it. He didn't know what a condominium was or why he had to move out so someone else could move in. He always paid his rent, even when he had to scrape it together, and he never caused problems. The whole thing didn't seem fair.

He crumpled the notice and unlocked the door.

His anger faded when he walked over to the couch and lifted the seat cushion. Underneath was a black revolver and a brown paper sack. Inside the bag was eighty-five hundred. One-fourth of the take from the drug rip the guys had pulled on Deuce, the self-proclaimed gateway to crank.

The money could buy Jace a new apartment, a bigger apartment, a better life.

Screw the eviction notice. Screw Antonio.

All he had to do was stay smart.

***

A knock on the door woke Jace. He had been sleeping on the couch. The money and gun were still under the cushions.

His apartment was one of the few in the building big enough for a couch. Unfortunately, that meant he had a Murphy bed attached to the nearby wall. He hated pulling the thing down, since it made the room feel small.

Someone knocked again, and Jace rolled off to his hands and knees. He was at eye level with the travel alarm clock on the coffee table. It was half-past one, and the sun shone through the windows.

He righted himself and stretched. There was another knock before he could get the door open.

Monroe stood there with his fist poised for another rap. "You look like hell." He dropped his hand and moved into the apartment.

With a push of his foot, Jace closed the door. "I was sleeping."

Monroe flopped onto the couch. He opened his mouth to say something but closed it. His eyes darted to the corner of the room.

"What?" Jace asked.

"Got a beer?"

Jace moved to the kitchen, but never looked away from the older man. He worried Monroe felt the gun and money underneath the seat cushion.

After giving him a beer, Jace asked, "So, you only came over for a cold one?"

Monroe took a long pull, then wiped his mouth with the back of his hand. "We need to talk about your partner."

"He's new to this." Even though he was pissed at Ricky, Jace didn't like anyone picking on him.

"It's more like he's new to pussy. Who's the woman?"

"Does it matter?"

"You know it does. If she figures out where Ricky got the money, we're all in danger."

Jace's stomach tightened, and he put the beer down.

"What's her name?"

"I dunno."

"Kid, don't be naïve. Lying about this makes you as stupid as him."

Jace's face warmed.

"You ain't going to tell me?"

"I'll find out who she is and what she knows. If I think she'll go to the cops, I'll tell you."

Monroe stood and watched Jace with weary eyes. "I'm not worried about the cops." He bumped Jace's shoulder on the way out.

***

Ricky stayed in the Carver Apartments, two blocks east of the Hope. He smiled when he opened the door.

"Where can I find Rochelle?" Jace asked.

Ricky's smile faded.

Previously, his friend had gossiped about this new girl, but Jace hadn't listened. The guy never had much success with women. Whenever one gave him any attention, he tended to lose his marbles. Women came and went and never stayed for very long. So Jace learned not to invest much time in learning about any woman that showed interest in Ricky.

"Why are you looking for her?"

"You know why."

Ricky's brow furrowed. "Is it really necessary?"

Jace cocked his head. He wanted to lash out and punch his friend but bringing Ricky in on the job had been his idea. The only one he could blame at this moment was himself.

Ricky lowered his head. "You can probably find her at The Well."

"She a bartender?"

"It's just where she drinks."

"What's she look like?"

"I already told you."

"I forgot."

"I'll go with." Ricky took a step into the hallway.

"No." Jace pushed him back into the apartment. "I'll talk to her alone. What's she look like?"

***

The Well sits at the corner of Second Avenue and Stevens Street.

Once inside, Jace waited for his eyes to adjust. After they did, he walked up to the bar and ordered a beer. The bartender, an unpleasant woman with stringy hair, didn't bother asking which type. She reached into a cooler, grabbed a can of Pabst, and cracked it open. "Two bucks."

Jace laid the exact amount on the bar. The bartender snatched the bills up without complaint.

He sat on a stool and casually surveyed the establishment. He usually didn't drink at The Well, but he saw a couple of guys he knew from around the way. They raised their cans in his direction. Jace nodded back.

There were three geezers at the rail, nursing their beers and grumbling amongst themselves. An elderly couple huddled together at a table.

In a back booth, a woman with ebony skin snuggled next to a pale guy in a tan suit. She matched Ricky's description. The suit didn't fit in with the establishment, however.

Jace made no secret that he watched them. The woman whispered to the guy, and he faced Jace. They studied each other for a moment before the man stood. He smoothed his pants, adjusted his jacket, then walked over.

"Got a problem?"

"She looks familiar."

The guy pulled Jace's beer away and slid it down the counter. "Looks like you're finished."

His face grew warm. "But I'm still thirsty."

Pulling his jacket to the side, the suit revealed a gun and a gold badge. Jace had seen the badge of the Spokane Police Department many times. This one did not look like that.

"Still thirsty?"

Jace slipped off his bar stool. "No, sir. I'm done."

***

Jace waited in the alley across the block. He thought about running back to his apartment to grab his gun, but he was worried Rochelle would leave while he was gone. Besides, Jace had never actually fired a gun, and knocking heads with a cop was plain stupid.

Stay smart, Jace repeated to himself. Stay smart.

That seemed to be half the battle in his life. Staying smart versus doing something dumb. Jace thought throwing in with Antonio and Monroe had been smart because they knew how to pull a job and make sure it would go smoothly.

Unfortunately, they let Ricky in the crew after Jace vouched for him. His friend screwed up afterward, and that made him Jace's responsibility. He needed to make sure the Rochelle thing wouldn't bite them all in the ass.

Jace was so wrapped up in his thoughts that he didn't hear the footsteps until it was too late. He spun around and now stood nose to nose with the man from the bar.

"Let me see your I.D."

"Are you a cop?"

He punched Jace in the stomach. "Your I.D."

Bent over and wheezing, Jace tugged his wallet out of his back pocket and handed it over.

The cop—Jace decided he would refer to him as one until he knew otherwise—slid his license free and threw the wallet back. Jace bobbled it before finally catching it.

"Jace Wheaton," the cop muttered. He then slipped the driver's license into a jacket pocket.

"That's mine."

The cop shoved Jace against the wall of a nearby building. "Where's the money?"

The words were so smooth and easy they caught Jace off guard. He opened the wallet and showed the five dollars inside. "It's yours if you want it."

The cop's lip curled. "Stop screwing around. Where is it?"

"I don't know—"

He slugged Jace in the gut.

Jace doubled over and sucked for air. The cop helped him upright, and Jace thought he was about to ask for the money again. Instead, the guy punched him once more. This time, Jace fell to the ground.

"I know about the rip, Jace Wheaton. Where's the money?"

"The money?"

The cop pulled his foot back, readying for a kick.

"Wait! Wait!" Jace said and lifted a pleading hand.

The cop didn't kick him but kept the foot ready. "Where's the money?"

"Are you really a cop?"

Jace puked after the guy kicked him in the side.

***

The cop drove Jace to the Hope.

They were in a newer Dodge, but it wasn't a police car. Jace struggled to think of all the jobs like cops—the ones that gave someone a badge and gun. He'd run across a lot of police, and none of them beat him as this guy did. Not out in the open, at least. This guy was something different.

Jace led the way into the apartments, past Dorothy at the front desk, and up to his apartment. The cop never said a word as they went.

At the door to his apartment, Jace said, "You're not a security guard."

"Open it."

Jace held his key just outside the lock. "And private investigators don't have a badge—"

The cop hit him in the ear with a cupped hand. "I've got a gun. What more do I need?"

At that moment, Jace figured the guy didn't need much more. He opened the door, and the cop shoved him in.

"Where's it at?"

"The couch." Jace stepped toward the piece of furniture.

The cop grabbed his shoulder and yanked him back.

"I'll look," he said and flipped up the cushions.

Only the gun was there.

The cop straightened and drew his gun. "Were you going to shoot me?"

Jace put his hands in front of him, as if trying to block the aim of the gun.

"The money was there. I promise."

The cop smacked Jace's hands out of the way. He lifted them back up, and the cop knocked them out of the way again.

"You thought you could ambush me?"

"No!"

The cop kicked him in the testicles and dropped Jace on the floor. He clutched himself as the cop squatted next to him. The gun barrel touched his temple. "You thought you could get the drop on me? Is that it?"

"The money was there," Jace groaned. "I swear."

The gun pressed harder into Jace's head.

"Who else is involved?"

Jace didn't even think about lying. "Antonio, Monroe, Ricky."

The cop tucked his gun away. He walked over to the couch and collected Jace's gun.

"I know about Ricky. Where can we find the other two?"

Jace stood but remained slightly hunched over as he cupped himself.

"Hey," the cop said, snapping his fingers. "Where can we find—"

"The Baker. They live there."

"Which one is tougher?"

The image of the older black man sitting on his couch popped into Jace's head. He had to have been the one to steal the money. "Monroe is tougher."

"Let's deal with him first."

***

The cop drove them to the Baker. Jace paid more attention to his car this time.

There wasn't a cop radio under the dashboard, and no other police paraphernalia floated around. Cops love their gadgets, and their cars are usually loaded with flashlights, expandable batons, and other do-hickeys. This guy didn't have any of that in his car. Instead, the only thing he had was a manual on liquor and cannabis laws. It was in the backseat.

"Are you with the liquor board?"

The cop eyed him, then glanced into the back. "Quit looking around."

At the Baker Apartments, he followed Jace up to Monroe's apartment. Every step led him to a new thought, and every new idea led Jace to believe Monroe came back to his apartment and stole his money. He'd definitely felt the cash when he sat on the couch.

Therefore, Monroe got Jace the beating from the liquor control agent. He hoped Monroe would get the same treatment.

The agent hid to the side while Jace knocked on Monroe's door.

"Whozit?" a voice came from the other side.

"Jace."

"Come in."

He opened the door and saw Monroe sitting at his kitchen table with a gun in his hand. "You alone?"

Jace walked into the apartment without shutting the door. "Yeah."

Monroe set the gun on the table. "Were you born in a barn?"

The agent walked in with his gun drawn.

"What the—" Monroe's hand hovered over his gun.

"Pick it up, and you're dead." The agent quietly shut the door.

The older man pulled his hand back and put it in his lap.

"Where's the money?" the agent asked.

Monroe's gaze flicked to Jace. "You told him?"

"He knew. Besides, you took mine."

"The hell are you talking about?"

The agent stepped closer to Monroe. "Where's your cut?"

"I don't know—"

The agent kicked Monroe in the shin.

"Shit!"

"Tell him where it's at," Jace said. "It only gets worse."

Monroe rubbed his leg. "The kitchen. Under the sink."

The agent reached out, took Monroe's gun from the table, and tucked it into the front pocket of his suit jacket.

He then walked into the kitchen and looked under the sink.

"You're dead for this," Monroe whispered to Jace. "You know that, right?"

"You stole my cut." As soon as the words left his mouth, Jace knew he sounded like a puss.

"Shut up, you two." From under the sink, the agent pulled out a brown paper bag and opened it. "How much is in here?"

"Eighty-five hundred," Monroe said.

"Where's the kid's cut?"

"I didn't take it."

"Bullshit!" Jace exclaimed.

"I didn't take it, kid. And why would you care? If I had it, he'd just take it, anyway."

The cop walked over to them. "You don't have the kid's money?"

"Nope," Monroe said.

"That's your final answer?"

"What else can I say?"

The agent smacked the barrel of his gun across Monroe's forehead. The older man crashed sideways into the table, then crumpled to the floor.

Jace jumped back from the unconscious form. The agent reached out and grabbed his arm. "Let's talk with the other one."

***

Antonio's apartment was another floor up.

Jace banged on the door a couple of times before it opened. When it did, the agent stuck his gun in the big Latino's face. Antonio never said a word as he backpedaled into the middle of the apartment. With each step he took backward, the agent took one forward. It was a crazy little dance.

"You're dead," Antonio growled at Jace without looking at him.

"Where's the money?" the agent asked.

"You a cop?"

The punch was so fast, Jace almost missed it. Antonio collapsed to the floor.

"Where's the money?"

Jace considered warning Antonio about lying, but he figured the man should learn the hard way, like he did.

The agent kicked Antonio in the stomach, flipping him over onto his back.

"Where's the money?"

Antonio held his belly with both hands.

"Grab his arm and hold it on the ground," the agent ordered.

Jace shook his head until the agent pointed the gun at him. Reluctantly, Jace grabbed Antonio's right arm and pinned it to the floor.

"Where's the money?"

The big man clawed at Jace with his free hand. "No!"

The agent drove the heel of his dress shoe onto the back of Antonio's hand.

Jace let go of the arm and scrambled away.

Antonio rolled over and tucked his broken hand under his body.

"I'll break the other one, too, unless you tell me where the money is."

The big man sucked for air and kept his hands under his body.

"Grab the other arm."

"Under the mattress!"

The agent walked over to the bed and flipped up the mattress. Underneath was another pile of bills.

"How much is here?"

"Eight grand," Antonio whispered. "Give or take." He had rolled himself over and was sitting upright, cradling his broken hand.

"You spent some of it?" Jace asked. "That's what Ricky did."

"Hey," the agent said. "Where's the kid's cut?"

Antonio looked at him. "Huh?"

"Someone stole my cut," Jace said. "Where's it at?"

"How would I know—"

The agent moved quickly and clubbed Jace with the barrel of his gun. He dropped to the floor and held his head.

"You lied!" the agent yelled.

"I didn't," Jace cried. He pulled a hand away to see blood on his fingers.

"Why don't I believe you?"

"I'd give it to you if I had it."

The agent chuckled mirthlessly. "Yeah, maybe. Maybe you would. Okay, here's what you're going to do. You're going to find that missing money because I'm coming by your apartment in the morning. If you don't have it, you know what'll happen…"

Jace nodded.

"Good," the agent said. "We have an understanding." He turned and left the apartment.

"You're dead," Antonio whispered.

"Blame Ricky. He told his girlfriend about the job."

"Fine." Antonio closed his eyes. "You're both dead."

Jace scrambled to his feet and headed for the door.

"Did you hear me?"

He pulled the door open and stepped into the hallway. "You're both dead!" Antonio yelled.

***

When the door to the elevator opened, Ricky was inside and flanked by two heavily tattooed thugs. Jace had seen one of them before when they pulled the drug rip. They were muscle for Deuce.

Ricky looked away like he didn't know Jace. Then he walked by with the two heavies in tow. Down the hallway, Ricky pointed at Antonio's door. "The rest of the money should be in there."

One of the thugs glared at Jace. "The fuck are you lookin' at?"

"Nothing." He hurried to the stairwell and yanked open the door. As he took the first step, someone kicked open the door to Antonio's apartment.

***

Jace sprinted back to the Hope, ran up the stairs to his apartment, and locked himself inside. He sat there with his back against the far wall.

His heart pounded as he tried to figure things out.

Ricky was with Deuce's thugs. They must have figured out who ripped him off. That meant they knew Jace was involved. Or did they? Ricky hadn't pointed him out when they got off the elevator. Maybe it was Ricky who took the money from Jace's apartment. Perhaps he did that to protect Jace.

That meant Ricky would have to get the rest of the money back from Monroe and Antonio, and they had already given it to the cop.

When Deuce's men didn't get the money, they would come back for Jace. Antonio or Monroe would surely sell him out. It was a bad idea for him to stay in his apartment.

He jumped to his feet and fled.

***

Jace lurked in alleys for the rest of the day and early into the night. He saw four cop cars and an ambulance outside the Baker. All of them had their emergency lights on.

He didn't bother to visit Ricky's apartment at the Carver Apartments. Deuce's crew could be there, waiting for him to show. He would have called Ricky if either of them had a phone.

When the sun went down, Jace went back to The Well. The bar was packed, and she sat alone at the counter. He sat on a stool next to her. Tiny diamonds sparkled in her lobes.

"Nice earrings," Jace said.

Rochelle studied him in the reflection of the mirror behind the bar. "That's a nasty gash on your head."

"Your boyfriend gave it to me."

"He can be rough when he doesn't get his way."

"He wants my cut, but I can't give it to him."

She grimaced. "That's going to hurt."

"I'd give it to him, but Ricky gave it to Deuce."

Rochelle sipped her drink. "Too bad."

"Yeah, *real* bad."

She set her drink on the counter and gave Jace a sideways glance.

"You told Deuce, didn't you?"

Rochelle rubbed her finger around the rim of her glass. "There was a finder's fee."

"What do you think they'll do when they find out your cop boyfriend has the money?"

"They'll let it drop. They won't go after him for that amount of money. It wouldn't be good for business."

"What about Ricky?"

"What about him?"

"What do you think Deuce will do with him?"

Rochelle shrugged a single shoulder. "I wouldn't want to be him."

"I thought you were his girlfriend."

"His girlfriend?"

"I thought you might actually care about him."

"Ricky was a means to an end."

"You're a bitch."

She leaned over and whispered, "I know two men that can make you disappear. You should be nice."

Jace lowered his eyes and turned away.

"That's better."

They sat there quietly while she sipped her drink. Jace considered ordering a shot but decided against it. His head still hurt from the pistol-whipping, and alcohol would probably make it hurt worse.

"Listen," Rochelle said, "my friend is going to be here soon, so unless you want another whooping—"

Jace slid off his stool and went outside.

He couldn't care less about Antonio and Monroe, but he worried about Ricky. He thought about trying to find him until he remembered Ricky was the reason everything went sideways.

Jace also remembered he was going to be evicted from his apartment soon. He didn't have much there, so there was no reason to go back.

He shoved his hands into his pockets and walked north toward the river. He didn't know where he was going, but he knew not to look back.

All he had to do was stay smart.

That was half the battle.

Daddy's Girl

With elbows resting on the dented brass rail, Loren Anderson held his head in his hands. Between his fingers, he rubbed his greasy hair, the result of two days without a shower. Below his face sat a Jack and Coke—his third since claiming this seat at the bar.

The Hole was a dirty stop along East Sprague Avenue, where the drunks escaped from the cold. It also provided the small neighborhood fish a corner to lurk whenever they needed to avoid the cops.

The stupid and arrogant fish—the ones who thought they were sharks—snapped up most police attention by driving shiny new Escalades and Yukons. The dangerous predators—the real sharks—wore suits and ties. They used words like revitalization and community reshaping. Loren had only been in town for three days and already witnessed the entire food chain in action.

A man in his early twenties with a misshapen afro slipped onto the stool next to Loren. He crossed his arms and looked straight ahead into the mirror behind the bar. After adjusting his North Carolina jersey, the man smiled at his reflection. Then he pulled his lips back and ran his tongue over his teeth. Loren thought the guy had the shifty glance that midlevel survivors on the food chain develop as a defense mechanism.

The younger man muttered, "Junior's on the way."

With a folded fifty in his fingers, Loren picked up his drink. After he swallowed the last bit, he set the glass on the bill and slid both toward his neighbor.

The kid placed one finger on a corner of the fifty and slid it from under the tumbler. He stuffed the bill into the front pocket of his jeans as he once more cleaned his teeth in the mirror. When he finished, he whispered, "Junior's for real. Best not to play around."

Loren studied his reflection. "I didn't pay for advice."

The younger man grunted and slid off the stool.

The bartender returned. He was a portly man with a flat-top haircut. His white T-shirt read *The Red Light District* and was splattered with the remains of a previous meal. On his meaty forearm was a USMC tattoo.

Loren tapped the counter next to his empty glass.

"You sure you can handle it?" The concern about his alcohol tolerance was cursory at best.

Loren tapped again.

The bartender shrugged and poured him another. Loren didn't touch it, though. He was already over his skis, and he knew better than to drink this one.

That didn't stop him from making a game out of it. For ten minutes, Loren mentally tortured himself. He wanted the drink but refused to take it. However, he silently encouraged himself to drink it but chastised himself for being weak whenever his fingers touched the glass. This game went on until the door to the bar opened, and Loren jerked his hand back.

He lifted his eyes to the mirror. The time for mental games was over.

Behind him, a large man crossed through the establishment. He wore an oversized winter coat and a stocking cap. He dropped heavily into a booth and slid across its seat.

Junior now held court.

The man lifted a hand, signaling he wanted a drink. The bartender acknowledged him with a nod. Almost immediately, visitors made their way for quick words. None stayed long, and they left the bar after that.

Loren watched the comings and goings until there was a break. He casually pushed away from the brass rail and walked over. Without asking for permission, he slid into the booth across from Junior.

The bigger man's lip curled. "Who the fuck you think you are?"

"A concerned citizen."

Junior's face relaxed. "Those are hard to come by down here—what we might call an endangered species."

Loren set his drink on the table.

"I didn't invite you to stay."

"It's a good thing I didn't ask."

Junior sniffed. Then he did it again. The second time was long and exaggerated, as he did it for the benefit of others. When he finished, his eyes narrowed. "You smell like a cop."

Loren remained silent. He had been one for more than twenty years until a constitutionalist strung out on rhetoric and Jim Beam ambushed him. Wrapping himself in conspiracy theories and the second amendment, the shooter attacked him with a stolen Kalashnikov. Loren took three rounds—one in the thigh, one in the shoulder, and one in the gut. When backup officers finally arrived, they killed the shooter in an exchange of gunfire that reminded Loren of his time as a soldier. When he got out of the hospital, he found he didn't have a taste for police work anymore.

"You're not one anymore, are you?" Junior gnawed on his lip. "What's stopping me from knocking your teeth through the back of your head?"

"Nothing."

"That's right—nothing."

"I've heard about you." Loren tried to sound stern. It had been many years since he'd come up against this type of man. "I've asked around."

"Best not to have my name in your mouth."

"People say—"

"They better not." Junior cocked his head. "Exactly, what are you after, old man? Wait. Don't tell me. Let me guess. You got a daughter."

Loren's eyes narrowed.

Junior slapped the table and laughed. "Goddamn if I didn't guess it. I've seen your kind down here before."

"My kind?"

"The white knight comin' to save his princess. Gonna kill me?"

"Depends."

He howled with laughter. "You know how many friends of mine are in here?"

"None."

He looked around and took stock of the patrons. "That a guess?"

Loren shook his head. "I'm a boy scout. I like to be prepared. The couple guys who might have been your friends left already. Now, it's just you. All by your lonesome." He lifted his glass and studied the booze in it. He felt the shake in his voice and wondered if the pimp had heard it.

Junior waved to the bartender, lifted two fingers, then gestured to their drinks. He did his best to keep an air of confidence, but Loren sensed some worry now emanating from the other man. He got used to smelling it in the war, but most of that came from his men.

"Which girl is yours?"

Loren frowned.

"Don't tell me. It doesn't matter. But I'm not guessin'. I've got too many of them to play that game."

"Marlene."

"Marlene?" Junior clicked his tongue against his teeth. "There's no Marlene in this game."

Loren sighed. Three weeks of searching for his daughter had taken its toll. He'd spent the last two days without sleep. He was to the point where annoyance replaced patience. "She goes by Rhonda now."

The bigger man held his hand in front of his mouth. "Oh, shit, Rhonda is yours? No wonder you want her back."

Loren's gaze dropped.

"Wanna diddle your baby girl one more time?"

"That was her real father. I'm her step."

The bartender put a fresh drink in front of the two men. Junior picked up his glass and swallowed the whole thing in a single pull. He winced as the alcohol went down. "She likes you."

"She was a good girl."

Junior snapped his fingers to pull Loren from the faint memories clouding his mind.

"She still is a good girl. She's the best producer I got."

Loren looked away as his face warmed.

"Relax, pops. She's a grown woman and can do what she wants."

"You got her strung out on that shit. She does what you want so she can continue to smoke."

"I didn't get her hooked on the rock. She did that all on her own in that white-bread world you raised her in. I only gave her a way to pay for it. And she's good at it. Maybe even the best."

Loren rubbed his face with his hands.

The door to the Hole opened, but Loren's features remained hidden by his hands. A pair of heels clicked over to the table.

"Dad?"

When Loren looked up, he fought back a rush of emotions. Marlene stood there with confusion in her eyes. She was no longer the little girl in jeans and pigtails waiting for a ride to Sunday school. Instead, she wore an old Navy Pea Coat over a skintight dress. Her skin was pale, and her legs were dirty. Her eyes looked as if they'd seen too much horror and one too many late nights.

"Hey, kiddo."

"What are you doing here?"

Loren's voice broke as he said, "I came for you."

"Why?"

He was taken aback by her question. "To bring you home."

She glanced at Junior, then shook her head. "I can't."

Loren motioned toward the pimp. "That's what we were talking about—him letting you go."

She faced Junior. "You want me to go?"

The pimp looked up at Marlene. His voice was low and smooth. "I want you to be happy, girl. If that means you go, then go. If that means you stay, then stay. But you make your choice. Him or me. It's simple."

When the pimp held her hand, Marlene's eyes softened.

Loren reached out and grabbed her arm. "You don't want this."

She bent down and kissed her father's cheek. "I love you," she whispered and pulled his hand from her arm.

Without looking at Marlene, Junior said, "Get back out there. Your father and me need to finish our talk."

She kissed Junior on the cheek and left without looking back. Both men watched her leave. When the door closed, the pimp turned to Loren.

"See how that works?"

Loren leaned forward. "I'm going to kill you."

Junior put his hand on the table. Underneath his palm was a small gun. "You should watch your tongue."

Loren dropped back into the booth and slowly lifted his hands.

"I own her."

"You don't—"

"I. Own. Her." He emphasized each word. "And when I'm done with her, I'll throw her away. You can have her back then, but don't clean her up too good because I may just want her back." His face was grim, but his eyes told the sad truth. "She'll come back, too. They always do."

Junior slid out of the booth and pocketed his gun. "You made your intentions clear, so let me make mine the same." His voice was loud, and everyone in the bar watched the two men. "If I find you anywhere down here, I'll have you beaten to within an inch of your life. There are guys down here who will do you for a dollar."

Loren stiffened.

A guy from somewhere in the bar yelled, "I'll do it for a fitty cent!"

"And if you ever approach me again," Junior continued, "I'll kill you." The bar fell silent. "No hesitation. No remorse. And no one in this joint will say one word about it."

The stares from the other patrons told Loren the truth.

Junior winked. "Have a nice day." Then he strolled out of the bar.

Loren sat alone, sipping his drink and allowing himself to get lost in his thoughts. There was nothing more to do now. Marlene made her choice. He'd seen enough of these moments while on the job. He could spend the rest of his life reaching out to her, but until she was ready to change, it wouldn't matter. The best thing he could do was go home and live his life. He would worry about her, of course. Maybe he should return to the church. It had been a long time since he prayed. He fought back the tears that welled in his eyes.

A young Asian woman entered the bar. She scanned the various patrons. When she found what she was looking for, she headed directly to Loren's table and slid into the booth across from him. She appeared barely twenty years of age, but her eyes were much older. Her winter coat hung below her shoulders, and she wore a yellow halter top.

They quietly watched each other for several moments.

"Junior send you?" Loren asked.

"Uh-huh. He said you wanted to be a daddy."

Loren stared at her with a growing tightness in his chest.

"You can be my daddy." She awkwardly licked her lips. "I promise to be a good girl. Unless that's not what you want. You can even spank me, but that's extra."

Now tears streamed down Loren's face.

The woman's face pinched. "Weirdo." She slid out of the booth. "You could have just said no."

Foolproof

"Quiet, or she'll hear us," Kerry whispered. He prepared to turn the doorknob with his left hand. A gun had come from somewhere and appeared in his other.

"Sorry," I whispered. My tongue had grown thick with fear. All I wanted to do was run away.

Kerry had told me this was going to be a burglary. The gun he now brandished showed me that his whole story had been a lie.

***

Kerry found me two weeks prior at the minimart.

He climbed out of an old Mazda 626 and strutted across the parking lot. As he neared the building, he lifted his sunglasses and pushed them back on his head, tucking long strands of blonde hair behind his ears.

The store's door opened with a chime. The multicolored strip hanging next to the door told me Kerry was six-foot-two, several inches taller than me.

He strode toward the beer cooler, his eyes never looking my way. He yanked open the door and grabbed a Budweiser tallboy. As he returned to the front, he snatched a small bag of Doritos from a nearby rack.

He set the items on the counter. "Gimme a hard box of Marlboro reds," he said in a nicotine-scarred voice.

I studied him briefly before reaching for the cigarettes.

Kerry dug into his pocket and pulled out a crinkled twenty. He tossed it on the counter and wiped his mouth.

"Still believe you're straight?" Even though we were the only two in the store, he whispered.

Old habits, I thought.

I nodded only once as I opened the register.

"Can I talk you into handing over the cash?"

I tucked his twenty into the appropriate slot, counted out the change, then closed the drawer with my hip. "Cameras," I muttered without looking toward the electronic eyes behind me and in the ceiling. "Besides, it ain't worth violating my parole. I need this job."

"That's the problem with parole, man. The system still has you by the balls."

"I know," I said and thought about all the times Kerry and I had sat in the yard at Walla Walla talking about when we would get outside. We were going to make a name for ourselves. I was there for accidentally killing a man while running from the cops. Kerry was there for robbing his third liquor store.

"You like it?" he asked.

"Doesn't have anything to do with like. You want that in a bag?" I tucked the beer, chips, and smokes into a small, brown paper sack.

Kerry grabbed his goods and dropped his sunglasses over his eyes. "I'll see you, Lou." He turned and strutted outside. With a plume of smoke, his car fired up, and he pulled out of the parking lot.

***

That night, I sat in my studio apartment and re-read an eviction notice I received months ago. I absently rubbed my St. Dismas medallion while my eyes drifted over the paper.

The Hope Apartments were being renovated, and the building's tenants were being tossed onto the street in twenty-seven days.

Why did I care? The building was nothing to brag about. Located in downtown Spokane, it was a dump, and my apartment was a dump inside a bigger dump.

I lived on the fourth floor with a view of the parking lot. Some apartments had views of the city to the south or the river to the north, but not me. Occasionally, I watched drug deals or a prostitute service a customer. Other than that, my view was of broken asphalt.

So, why did it matter that I was getting evicted with all the others? Maybe because, once my freedom was taken away, I felt the need to protect it. Getting kicked out made me feel powerless.

The only thing I had of any value was the St. Dismas medallion. Dismas was a thief and hung on a cross next to Christ. He was now the patron saint of prisoners. After my conviction, my father gave it to me. He said he would pray for me every day. Unfortunately, he died while I was in prison.

My thumb traced the edge of the medallion as I stared at the eviction notice. I was no longer reading it, though.

It didn't seem fair. I was staying straight. I didn't want to go back to prison. Some guys liked that life, but for me, incarceration was what the system hoped it would be. It was a hell I never wanted to repeat.

But seeing Kerry walk into the store looking happy and carefree bothered me.

I wasn't happy.

And I sure as fuck wasn't carefree.

***

A few days later, Kerry showed up again at the minimart. He came in with the same strut and the same sunglasses pushed on top of his head. He never made eye contact as he headed back to the beer cooler and pulled out another tallboy.

Kerry walked up to the counter when the other customers left and laid another crinkled twenty on it.

"Interested in doing some work outside of here?"

"No," I said flatly and shoved his beer into a bag.

As I dug into the register for his change, Kerry leaned in. "Five grand for an hour's work."

"Sounds like a felony. My freedom's worth more than that."

"I'll let you think about it before taking your answer as gospel."

He snatched the brown paper bag and strolled out of the store.

***

That night, Kerry showed up at my apartment. I was surprised to see him standing there. He wore a big grin and carried a six-pack of Miller in his hand.

"Wanna share some of the high life?" He lifted the beer to emphasize his joke.

I stepped out of his way and let him in.

He glanced around. "Nice place. How long you been here?"

"Since I got out."

"What's that been? Six months?"

"Seven."

"Seven months. Man, that's awesome. I've been out for almost thirty days now."

Kerry walked over to the little kitchen table and its one chair. He set the beers on the table and saw the eviction notice sitting on it. He slid the paper over with a finger and nodded as he read.

"Where you staying?"

"With my baby's momma."

"I thought you said you couldn't trust her."

"I can't," he said with something close to a shrug. His eyes were still on the eviction notice. "She's a slut, but I needed a place to stay." When he looked up, he added, "But I can bang her like the next guy, and I don't have to pay no rent."

When we were incarcerated, he talked about his girlfriend constantly. Half the time, he groused about her. The other times he sounded sad. It surprised me to hear he'd gone back. Regardless, he didn't have to worry about eviction.

Kerry slipped one of the beers from its carrier and handed it to me. He pulled one for himself. After opening the bottle, he raised it for a toast. I performed the same action and tapped mine against his, not knowing what good fortune we had to celebrate.

He slurped his beer and grimaced when he swallowed. "Okay, Lou, let's talk business."

I sat on the ratty recliner, and it squeaked under my weight. "I ain't doing nothing that will land me back in there."

"This is easy."

I shook my head.

"And foolproof."

"Nothing is foolproof."

Kerry sipped his beer again. "There's this old broad on the South Hill who is loaded beyond belief. She's widowed, so there's no man around the house. Ain't no dogs, either. It's ripe for the taking."

"Why are you doing this? You want to go back?"

Kerry pointed at me. "I ain't afraid of it, if that's what you're asking."

"That's not what I'm asking."

He ran his fingers through his hair. "I'm not going to work for minimum wage. I'm better than that."

"Fuck you, man."

Kerry's smile was soft, almost apologetic. "I'm not saying you're doing something wrong by jockeying a register, but that ain't me."

"Again, fuck you."

"Okay, okay," he said, raising his hands in surrender. "I'm sorry. Listen, I know a guy who knows a guy who wants us to hit this broad."

"Hit?"

Kerry raised his hand to stop me. "I meant rob."

"Why?"

"Because she stole some land from him."

I thought about how someone would go about that. "How do you steal land?"

"Through the courts, I guess. They prolly do that shit all the time. You know as well as anyone the system is crooked and set up for the rich."

"We all know that, but how do you steal land?"

"Do I look like a judge? How the hell should I know? All I do know is this guy is willing to give us ten grand to go in there and clean her out. That's five apiece, mi amigo."

"What does he get out of it?"

"Whatever we take, we give to him. And I have a shopping list of places to look and things to take."

It sounded fishy, so I sipped my beer, buying time to think of more questions. Finally, I asked, "How'd this guy find you?"

Kerry shrugged. "Like I said, a friend of a friend. He was looking for someone, and my friend got word to me."

"Who's the guy? And who's your friend?"

"That's not how this works."

There was no point in arguing. Kerry had his own set of crazy rules, and I wouldn't get him to break them. He was solid in that way. He would never sell out a friend, but that didn't mean he wouldn't take advantage of one if he could.

"Why come to me about this?"

"You owe me. Remember?"

Of course, I remembered. Kerry came to my rescue in the pen when the white-power types braced me. I would have fought them, but in the end, no one beat that group. He got them to leave me alone.

"I'll never forget, but I was straight before I went in, and I want to stay straight now."

Kerry ran his finger around the lip of his beer can. "How about revenge? Can I interest you in a little of that?"

"Revenge? On who?"

"Veronica Caldwell."

"Who the hell is Veronica Caldwell?"

Kerry tapped the eviction notice on the table. "She's the woman evicting you."

"No, she's not."

"Trust me. I read about her in the newspaper."

I lifted the eviction notice. "Her name isn't on this. Don't you think it should be here? All they got is some property manager guy."

"Don't believe me then. But ask yourself this—what do I get by lying to you?"

"Wait." I went searching for my lease. I found it in a folder in a kitchen drawer. At the head of the paperwork, where the field asked for the landlord's name, was a handwritten Clinton and Veronica Caldwell. "Son of a bitch."

"You see," Kerry said in triumph. "I know what I'm talking about."

***

Later that night, as I lay on the lumpy mattress that came with the apartment, I wondered about Veronica Caldwell.

Who was she?

What kind of person had the kind of power to evict an entire building?

What did she think about when she lay in bed at night? Whatever it was, I was sure she wasn't worried about being evicted from her home.

***

Kerry showed up at the store the next day. The Mazda still burned oil, but he looked happy as could be when he strolled in. He stepped inside the door and stared at me with a look of expectation.

I was ringing up a customer, and there were two more waiting in line.

Kerry asked, "Well?" when I finally glanced in his direction.

I nodded, and he snapped his fingers.

"All right," he muttered, then left the store.

I finished ringing up the customers, leaned on the back counter, and sighed.

***

It was after 11:30 on Thursday night when we headed up to Veronica Caldwell's. She lived on Rockwood Boulevard, where the garages were larger than the apartment that I lived in.

I didn't want to do the job at night. She would likely be home, but the guy paying us for the job wanted it done while she was asleep. According to Kerry, a burglary wasn't as dramatic if she came home to it after it had been done. The whole thing seemed stupid, but when Kerry gave me the pitch, I bought it.

I bought it because I *wanted* to buy it.

Kerry spotted her house but drove past it. It was a massive structure—two levels and so wide it seemed like a couple of places smushed together. We went another block before Kerry pulled to the side and turned off the engine.

He glanced at me. "Still okay?"

I rubbed St. Dismas and nodded.

"Let's go." Kerry climbed out of the car.

***

The house was alarmed, but Kerry had the security code to the three-car garage. When I asked him how he got it, Kerry said his friend of a friend had done his homework.

"This will be the easiest money either of us makes."

Kerry tapped in the four-digit code, and the garage door slid up slowly and quietly. It went down just as silently. Leave it to the rich to have stealth-like garage door openers.

The garage connected with the house, but the inner door was locked. Kerry pulled out a black pouch of tools and handed me a small flashlight. I held the beam on the doorknob while he set to work on the lock. It took him a few minutes to get it open, but it finally gave.

We stepped inside the house and found ourselves in the kitchen. I gently closed the door and handed Kerry the flashlight.

He had a map of the house that went along with his laundry list of items to get.

"Let's tie her up first."

"What?" I tried hard to keep my panicked voice to a whisper.

"We can't afford to have her catch us. This will take a while."

"That wasn't part of the plan."

I turned to go back to the garage, and Kerry snatched my arm. "Listen, amigo. You owe me. And if you walk out now, you get nothing. I'm not talking about killing the woman, just tying her up until we're done."

I stared at Kerry until I believed what he said. We weren't going to hurt the woman. We only needed more time to do the job. It made sense.

"All right," I agreed.

***

We moved slowly and soundlessly through the house, using the map as a guide. Her bedroom was on the second floor. We carefully took a flight of stairs, which never creaked once.

Kerry stopped abruptly, and I bumped into him, almost knocking him over. "Shit," I blurted.

"Quiet, or she'll hear us." He prepared to turn the doorknob with his left hand. A gun had come from somewhere and appeared in his other.

"Sorry," I whispered. My tongue had grown thick with fear. All I wanted to do was run away. "What's the gun for?"

"To scare her."

Tying her up wasn't part of the plan, and neither was the gun.

Kerry held up three fingers, and then he dropped them one by one until there were none. When he opened the door, I realized we had nothing with which to tie up the woman.

He crouched as he moved into the room. I followed him and hunkered low in the darkness. Kerry pointed his small flashlight toward the bed. I breathed a sigh of relief to find it empty. It was neatly made and hadn't been slept in.

Kerry turned toward me with a confused look. He pulled out his map of the house and studied it. "Where the hell is she?" He straightened and shoved the map back into his pocket. "We need to find her."

"Maybe we got lucky, and she's out for the night."

"We need to find her," he repeated. His voice filled with panic.

"Why?"

Kerry waved me off and hurried into the hallway. I stayed behind and took a final look around the bedroom. Why was he acting so—

A shotgun blast shook the house. Kerry appeared briefly in the doorway, stumbling backward, then he crumpled to the floor.

I ducked behind a big wooden dresser. I struggled to swallow as my throat suddenly seemed to close in on itself.

"I know you're in there," an elderly woman said.

My heartbeat was in my ears now, and I looked for an escape route. The window was the only option, but we were on the second floor, and I had no idea what was below.

"If you come out, I'll shoot you." There wasn't any fear in her words.

"I'll stay put until the cops get here!" My voice sounded like it was coming from the bottom of a well. I moved toward the window, hoping to escape.

"Who put you up to this?"

"I don't know," I said over my shoulder.

"Was it my youngest?"

I looked through the window and considered the drop to the ground. There were bushes below with a small fence protecting them from the rest of the yard. Landing on that might impale me.

"He sent you boys, didn't he?" Her voice remained steady and strong.

My hands shook as I unlatched the window and tried to lift it. The damn thing didn't budge. I looked closer at the windowsill. It was painted shut.

"Are you working for my son?"

How was she not afraid?

I spun around, looking for something to pry the window open. There was nothing except a big book on the nightstand. I picked it up and was about to throw it through the glass when she said, "If you throw that, I'll shoot you. I rather like that window."

I glanced back and saw an elderly woman holding a shotgun in the doorway. I carefully set the book on the nightstand.

"I don't want to hurt you," she said.

"Then let me go."

"That wouldn't be right."

She cradled the gun confidently. "Don't worry. I'm pretty handy with this thing. That's the benefit of having a father who liked to bag ducks. Why don't you sit down, and we'll wait for the police together?"

I sat on the bed.

"Why did you come here?"

"My friend asked me."

"You came to kill an old woman because a friend asked you?"

"We were only going to rob your house."

"And you believed that?"

I nodded.

"Why'd you come to this particular house?"

"Someone came to Kerry." I motioned toward the body on the floor. "He made the deal."

"Did you meet that someone?"

I shook my head.

"Why go along then?"

"Revenge."

"Revenge?" Her voice rose in curiosity. For the first time, she seemed to have heard something she didn't expect.

"You're evicting me from the Hope."

"Oh, a vendetta. Tell me—how long is your parole?"

"Huh?"

"There are only two types of people who live there—ex-convicts and mental patients. You don't look crazy to me."

"Thirty-six months."

"Three years of parole. You must have done something bad. This won't go well for you when the police show up."

I could hear sirens in the distance.

"It will be bad." I lowered my head and stared at my shoes. Tears welled in my eyes as I thought of more years in prison. And that wasn't even taking into consideration the extra time for what we did that night.

"What's your name?"

I told her.

"Want a way out, Lou?"

Images of prison blazed in my mind. "Yes," I said flatly. "Whatever you want."

***

I don't know what she told the police because I was gone before they arrived. I strolled out of the house and tried to look like a man with all the time in the world. My walk home gave me time to think about the events of the evening.

It was late the following Saturday night when I strode up to a large house in the Blackstone development. A place like that costs more money than I'd see in a lifetime, and the neighborhood was lousy with them.

I rang the bell, and after a few moments, the door opened slightly. In the crack, I could see a man in his late forties. He had a round face with small eyes behind big reading glasses. The hair on his head was thinning.

"Yes?"

"Alvin Caldwell?"

He looked me up and down. "Who's asking?"

"One of the guys you hired."

His eyes narrowed. "What do you want?"

"The money you promised."

"You didn't hold up your end of the bargain."

"Things happen," I said.

"You made a mess of the whole affair. You're not getting a cent."

"My friend is dead. Pay me, or I tell the cops."

He thought about it before stepping back from the door. "My family will be home soon."

"You don't have a family."

"How do you—"

"Get the money."

His eyes searched mine. "Wait here."

I grabbed his arm. "I'll go with you."

Alvin hesitated before leading me to a back room. He opened a closet door to reveal a safe on the floor. "The money's in there."

"Get it."

He unlocked the safe and pulled out a small white envelope. "This is the ten grand I promised your friend."

I took the envelope and flipped it open. Cash was stuffed inside.

"Ten grand is a lot for a robbery."

Alvin's face scrunched. "Robbery? Why would I want you to rob her?"

I tucked the envelope into my back pocket. "Yeah. Why would you want that?"

He closed the safe and stood, brushing his pants as he did. "How'd you know it was me that hired you guys? I thought I was—"

"Careful? Your mother told me where to find you."

His eyes locked onto the gun I now held. Veronica gave it to me. It was one of her father's.

I don't know what kind of man would want to kill his mother. For that matter, I couldn't comprehend the type of woman who could coldly manipulate the murder of one of her sons.

But they're the rich, and they're a wholly different species than the rest of us.

Alvin Caldwell's mouth opened and closed slowly, like a dying fish.

Six years ago, I accidentally killed a man.

Tonight, it wouldn't be an accident.

Death at Sunrise

The cell phone vibrated on the nightstand next to Shane McAfee's head. His eyes fluttered open, and he lazily reached out for it.

He closed his eyes again and answered the call. "McAfee," he whispered.

"Shane? It's Laura."

He was silent for a moment before she continued.

"There's a suspicious death we need you on."

"It's Saturday," Shane muttered.

"So? You're next on the rotation. The captain says you're flying solo. There's a double homicide in Rockford, so we're stretched thin. And since your call looks like a suicide, he thought you could handle it on your own."

He absently caressed the naked hip of the woman lying next to him.

"Shane?"

He blinked a couple of times at the morning sunlight streaming in through the blinds. The room had a hazy glow to it. "Where's it at?" he asked.

"The Sunrise Camp for Boys and Girls."

"It's a kid?"

"A teenager."

"Shit," he said and ended the call.

Shane rolled over and stared into the sleeping face of the woman next to him. Emily had recently celebrated her twenty-first birthday. He was closing in on his thirty-fifth. In the department's eyes, their age difference wasn't even the worst part of this relationship. It had been a bad decision to get involved with her. It was a worse decision to stay involved.

"Wake up," he whispered.

Emily rolled onto her side and exposed herself. Her eyes remained closed against the morning light. She gently touched Shane's chest and softly moaned.

"I need to go," he said.

"Why?"

"Work."

She snaked her hand around Shane's waist and pulled herself to him. His body instinctively reacted.

"Stay with me," she said with a dreamy smile.

"I can't. There's been a death."

"Yuck," she said and flopped onto her back.

Shane stood. "My sentiments exactly."

***

It took Shane almost thirty minutes of driving before he pulled into a dirt parking lot in front of several brown buildings. The Sunrise Camp for Boys and Girls was located at the northeastern tip of Shelby Lake, about thirty miles north of Spokane.

His clothes were the same as he'd worn at the office yesterday: a black suit, a wrinkled white shirt, and a scuffed pair of black loafers. A tie was folded and tucked into the left jacket pocket. His gun was secured in a hip holster, and his badge was attached to his belt.

Shane had visited the camp years before while he was still a deputy. Back then, a young camper had gone missing. After a couple of hours of searching, they found the kid lost and scared in the woods. Shane would have given a day's pay to be there for the same reason.

When he turned his car off, the radio station fell silent, abruptly interrupting a Dierks Bentley song.

"Took your sweet time, McAfee."

He glanced over to see Sergeant Irvin Lee approaching.

"Must have been out late last night at the clubs," Lee snickered at him. He mimed some dance moves as he walked. "Or wait, maybe you went to Chuck E. Cheese instead?"

Shane ignored the comments and rolled up his window. He'd been getting a lot of crap since word got around about Emily. When he exited his car, he said, "Want to show me what you found?"

Lee motioned for him to follow, and they headed toward a dirt path. The path was thin and disappeared into the nearby woods. A young deputy stood at the beginning of the path. Shane nodded as they walked by.

The two men followed the path as it dropped down near the waterline. On the left was a steep hillside speckled with smaller cabins. Each structure had a set of wooden stairs that ran to the path. On the right was Shelby Lake.

Shane silently followed Lee until the sergeant stopped and pointed at a small structure on the hill. "The victim's cabin."

"He up there?"

"No."

"Anybody I.D. him yet?"

"His name's Nathan Price. Eighteen years old."

"I thought this was a camp for little kids."

"Relax, McAfee. In a couple more years, they'll be in your dating range."

Shane spun around and glared at the sergeant. "Get off my back."

Lee lifted his hands in mock surrender and chuckled. "Relax, pretty boy. We all can't date a celebrity."

"You two knock it off," Lieutenant Max Reisdorf said as he neared.

Lee thumbed toward Shane. "Your boy can't take any—"

Reisdorf stepped between the two men. "Irv, go up top and wait for the coroner."

The sergeant frowned. "It's his problem if he can't take a joke."

"The parking lot," the lieutenant said flatly.

Sergeant Lee grumbled something as he ambled off toward the camp's entrance. When he was out of sight, Shane faced the lieutenant.

"I appreciate that, El Tee."

"Don't thank me. I'm as pissed as he is. I just don't joke about it."

The detective blew out a breath of air. "Hey, why are you here, Lieutenant? If this is a simple suicide, then Lee and I can handle it. Not that I'm ungrateful for your presence."

Reisdorf put his hands on his hips. "It's a camp full of kids. When word gets out, it's going to bring the newshounds. Someone needs to be here for a little public relations, and Lee's not exactly our best foot forward."

Shane smiled. "He's definitely not that."

"He's still a helluva lot better than you right now."

The detective's smile faded.

"Want some advice, McAfee? Quit messing with the mayor's daughter. It'll make us all happier."

Emily was the daughter of the Spokane Valley mayor. The city had a contract with the County Sheriff's office to provide police services to the municipality. Supposedly, the mayor's recent anger toward the sheriff and the department was a direct result of the detective's relationship with his daughter. Everyone seemed to have developed this idea when the mayor reportedly yelled at the sheriff, "Keep Detective Loverboy away from my baby girl!"

Shane opened his mouth to protest, but Lieutenant Reisdorf cut him off. "But you aren't about to do that, are you?"

"My personal life is—"

"That's where the kid was staying." The lieutenant said and pointed toward the nearby cabin.

"Lee already told me that."

Reisdorf raised his eyebrows.

"But what he didn't tell me was why an eighteen-year-old kid is out here at summer camp."

"The boy was an advisor."

"An advisor? What's that mean?"

"It means he advises. How the hell do I know what it means? He stayed up in that cabin, is what I know. It's taped off now, and one of ours is up there sitting guard on it."

Shane looked around and realized how quiet the camp was. "Where is everybody?"

"The advisors and additional staff were rounded up. They're sitting in the cafeteria waiting for you." Reisdorf checked his watch. "To make matters worse, it's almost nine. The kids arrive in less than an hour."

"They arrive today?"

Reisdorf crinkled his nose.

"How many?"

"Two hundred."

"Shit."

"Tell me about it. We've been waiting the better part of an hour for you to bring your ass out here."

"I was delayed."

Reisdorf frowned. "We all know what delayed you, and we don't like it. We don't like it one bit."

"You want me to leave? You can call someone else out—"

"Stop being a baby. You brought this on yourself. You had to know people weren't going to accept it."

He had suspected it, but he went through with it, anyway. And he should have broken it off weeks ago, but he couldn't bring himself to do that. He did what he shouldn't and avoided what he should. He was acting like a teenager.

The lieutenant must have known what he thought because he harrumphed, shook his head, and muttered, "Let's go."

***

The two men walked down the path until they came to a clearing covered in dirt and sand. There was a view of the water, and sunlight shimmered on the lake.

On the far side of the clearing was a dock that jutted into the water. The path that brought them to the clearing continued to the opposite side and disappeared into thicker foliage.

Reisdorf pointed up. "There he is."

Shane followed the lieutenant's finger, then quickly stepped back. Hanging from a large tree branch was a young man in a dirty white T-shirt and khaki shorts. "Why isn't he cut down?"

"How do you propose we do that?"

Shane stared at Reisdorf.

"He's too high for us to get at."

The detective looked back up. "Well, how did he get up there?"

"The rope swing starts there." Reisdorf pointed to a perch on the hillside. "They launch themselves over this clearing and out onto the water."

Shane imagined the arc of the swing and someone letting go of the rope to fall into the lake. "How do they get the rope back after they jump?"

The lieutenant pointed at the kid's foot. A smaller rope was tangled around his ankle. "They have a thinner rope tied to the main line. That's what they used to get the rope to the next kid."

"Is he going to hang up there until his head pops off?"

The lieutenant grimaced. "The coroner is on the way. And we asked forensics to bring some ladders along with them."

Shane moved around the clearing to study Nathan Price. The teenager hung roughly nine feet above the ground. The rope was almost still, but the kid's body turned slightly in the breeze. If anyone climbed up onto the large branch to cut the rope, the kid would fall several feet before someone would have the chance of catching him. Too much evidence would be destroyed.

The detective slowly walked up the hillside toward the rope swing's perch. The dirt along the area looked freshly disturbed. Shane stopped to examine Nathan's dirty T-shirt. He wished he could get closer.

"Anyone take pictures of this trail?" There were random footprints in the rocky dirt, but nothing that seemed out of the ordinary.

"One of the deputies got some pictures, but I'll have forensics take additional."

Shane continued up the path, taking care not to disturb any potential footprints. He stopped at the jump-off point for the rope swing. The dirt appeared compacted except for a few non-descript footprints. Twenty-five feet further up the hill and around the tree was another small perch with disturbed dirt.

"How about up here?"

Reisdorf looked up at Shane. "Yeah, we got pictures up there, too."

The small perch was closer to the tree and higher than the jump-off point. This perch would not allow someone to swing out over the clearing. Instead, it would be likely they would fall until the rope pulled tautly.

Shane said, "He went from up here where there was more slack in the rope."

"That's what we were thinking."

The tree stood at the edge of the perch, and Nathan Price hung several feet from where Shane now stood. With his hand holding onto the tree for balance, the detective leaned forward over the drop. He studied Nathan as best he could. Shane saw red in Nathan's hair.

"Looks like he was hit in the back of the head."

"What?"

He pushed away from the tree and stood upright. "The kid was hit in the back of the head with something. Have the guys fan out and look around for a weapon, maybe a rock or something."

Reisdorf waved his hand about. "Everywhere you look, there are rocks, bigger rocks, and other heavy things. That's a bunch of possibilities."

Shane shrugged but kept his eyes on Nathan Price. "Then they need to get started."

***

When Shane headed back toward the parking lot, he caught a whiff of Emily's soap on his skin. He wished he was still in bed with her.

The morning sun brought an unseasonably warm heat with it. Beads of sweat formed on his forehead as he continued along the path.

He stopped at the stairs leading up to Nathan Price's cabin. Shane was in good shape, but he was disappointed to breathe so heavily after walking up the path.

Grabbing the handrail, he pulled himself onto the first step. Twenty-six steps later, he walked onto the wooden sidewalk that led to the fourth cabin. A young deputy leaned on a column supporting the porch roof. He immediately straightened when he saw Shane.

"Sir?" he said.

"Detective McAfee," he said with a nod. "Anybody been in there?"

"The lieutenant and me made a quick sweep."

"Anybody take pictures inside?"

"No, sir."

Shane thought about waiting for a deputy with a camera or the forensics team but decided that he would record it later in his report if he found anything. "I'm going in for a look. Call for a camera."

The detective stepped by him then and entered the cabin. As he did so, his eyes swept top to bottom, left to right, searching for anything that might help him. He noticed the place smelled like Pine-Sol.

The room was a large bay with ten bunk beds, five on each side of the room. The mattresses were bare, and the floor recently swept. On both sides, located between the second and third bunks, were desks.

Children would soon fill the empty camp, and the order and cleanliness of this moment would be lost for the summer.

Shane walked to the rear of the cabin and found two smaller rooms. One was a bathroom with two stalls, two showers, and two sinks.

Across from the bathroom was the second room. A simple plaque hung on the door. It read *Advisor*.

The door was slightly ajar. Shane peeked through a crack between the door and the frame before slowly pushing it fully open. He was careful not to touch the metal doorknob.

The room contained a single bed. The top sheet was rolled back neatly over the edge of the bedspread. A single pillow rested at the top of the bed. In the corner of the room was a desk with a laptop computer. Shane checked the computer and found it turned off.

Near the head of the bed was a dresser. Shane pulled open each of the drawers by their edges and found underwear and socks in the top drawer, shorts and T-shirts in the second drawer, and the bottom drawer contained jeans. All the clothing was neatly folded.

When Shane glanced around the room again, he noticed how the sunlight highlighted the floor. It was freshly swept. The whole room was very tidy.

He got on his hands and knees and found a pair of flip-flops under the bed. He then searched between the mattress and metal support wires but found nothing. Shane pushed himself to his knees and leaned on the bed.

"Damn," he muttered and started to stand. He stopped, though, and flipped the pillow over. Underneath was a folded piece of paper.

"Damn," Shane muttered again.

He unfolded it and read the words it contained. Shane laid the paper on the bed and pulled out his notebook. He quickly copied the letter's content.

When he finished, he refolded the paper and placed it under the pillow. After a final glance around the room, he went outside.

"Hey," he called to the young deputy. "Is the camera on the way?"

"Yes, sir. Forensics will take care of it when they get here."

Shane thumbed toward the cabin. "There's a letter under the pillow of the advisor's bed. I didn't touch anything else."

The detective headed toward the stairs.

"Well?" the deputy called. "What did the letter say?"

Shane stopped and glanced back. "It said he killed himself."

***

He took his time walking back up the path. His thoughts were on the letter and what it meant. When he found a deputy standing at the path's entrance, he said, "Do me a favor and call Lieutenant Reisdorf. Ask him to meet me up here."

The deputy nodded in acknowledgment and reached for his shoulder microphone.

Shane walked into the large grassy area and lifted his face to the sun.

"Are you the detective?"

He blinked a couple of times at a skinny man in a blue polo shirt and khaki shorts. His shirt was neatly tucked, and the khakis were recently ironed. His brown hair was short and combed precisely. The man stood roughly equal in height to Shane's six feet. He stuck his hand out and waited for Shane to take it.

"That's right," Shane said and shook his hand.

"I'm David Palmer, the camp's director. I can't believe this is happening."

"These things can be upsetting."

"It most certainly is." Palmer then pointed to the parking lot. "Any moment the buses are going to arrive. I need to know what to do."

"Send them home."

Palmer's eyes widened as he shook his head. "I can't do that."

"Why?"

"Because the Sunrise Camp provides services for various churches and organizations. The groups coming for this session are from as far away as Walla Walla and Moses Lake. Their ride here is almost four hours."

The detective shrugged. "Unfortunately, I can't have the kids running around while we complete our investigation. When the buses arrive, have them park in the lot. Don't let the kids come into the camp until I tell you."

Palmer looked as if he'd bitten into a lemon. "What about food and water?"

"Are you out?"

"No, we have plenty. But I need help getting it to the children."

"I'll do what I can to clear some advisors. Will that help?"

The camp director sighed. "I guess it'll have to do."

"Now, let me ask you a couple questions."

Palmer's eyes focused on the detective.

"Who called to report the kid's death?"

"I did—from my office. Most cell phones won't work out here."

Shane pulled his phone from his pocket. The screen showed no service.

"How did you find the kid's body?"

Palmer shook his head. "I didn't find him. Mark Brown did."

"Mark Brown?"

"He's an advisor. Stays in cabin three."

"So, Mark Brown finds Nathan Price hanging in the tree and comes running to you?"

"That's what he told me. Yes. We immediately called the police."

"Using the phone in your office?"

Palmer nodded.

"Did you go down and see the body?"

"I did. Afterward. It was very sad."

Shane glanced around before asking, "So where is Mark Brown now?"

"He and the rest of the staff are in the cafeteria." Palmer pointed at a long, brown building.

Behind the cafeteria was the administration building. Shane had noticed it on the way in. The building to the east was a small brown affair. Behind it were two smaller buildings. Shane pointed at them. "What's in those buildings?"

"The furthest is the maintenance shed. The closer one is the nurse's office."

"Are there computers in any of the buildings?"

"There's a computer in the nurse's station, one in my office in the admin building, and one in the lounge of the cafeteria building."

"Can the advisors use any of those?"

Palmer shook his head. "They can only use the computer in the cafeteria building. The one in the admin building is used only by me. The nurse's station is locked and for the nurse only."

Shane rubbed his chin and felt a day's worth of stubble. "Do me a favor and ask Mark to come out and talk with me. No one except you can leave the cafeteria at this time. Understood?"

"Yes, sir," Palmer said and hurried off to the cafeteria.

Shane pulled out his notebook and made a few entries.

***

With a sheen of sweat on his forehead, Lieutenant Reisdorf walked up to Shane. "You sent for me?" Irritation was evident in his voice.

"I checked out the kid's cabin." Shane tucked the notebook back into his pocket. "I found a letter under his pillow."

"What'd it say?"

Shane watched the cafeteria building as he spoke. "It said Nathan was sorry for touching little boys. He couldn't take the guilt and decided to kill himself."

"That settles it."

The detective frowned. "How do you figure?"

"The kid left a suicide note."

"What about the blood on the back of his head?"

"He probably cracked it against the tree after he jumped and swung around a bit."

Shane shrugged. "There's still the problem with the note."

Reisdorf put his hands on his hips. "And what problem might that be?"

"The suicide note was done with a computer printer."

"And?"

"There's no printer in his room or his cabin."

Reisdorf crossed his arms over his chest.

"That's what I thought." Shane fought back a smug smile. "I'm going to need a couple things."

"Tell me it doesn't involve manpower. I'm stretched thin as it is."

"I need someone to secure the computer in the cafeteria."

"Of course," Reisdorf muttered. "Where am I going to get more people?"

Shane shrugged. "You'll figure it out. That's why you're the lieutenant."

"Anything else?"

"I need someone to check out all the other cabins to see if anyone has a computer and printer inside."

"That'll take some time."

"I've got plenty of time." Shane pointed to several buses pulling into the parking lot. "But those kids are going to get pretty restless sitting in those sardine cans."

***

Mark Brown was a good-looking kid. His angular features, bushy brows, and dark eyes were the type young girls would probably fawn over. He had the athletic build of a football player: tall, muscular, and lean. He wore a bright white T-shirt that read *Sunrise Camp* and khaki shorts. On his feet were a pair of flip-flops.

His eyes were nervous, though, as he approached Shane. "Mr. Palmer said to see you."

Shane waved for Mark to follow, and the two walked over to a picnic table in the grassy area, out of sight from the buses.

"Grab a seat."

Mark slowly sat, his eyes never leaving the detective.

Shane pulled out his notebook and laid it on the table. "You found Nathan this morning?"

Mark nodded.

"And then you reported it immediately to the camp director?"

"That's exactly what I did."

"Tell me how you found Nathan."

"I was heading toward the cafeteria to get breakfast, and I saw him hanging there."

"What time was this?"

"About eight."

Shane made a quick entry in his notebook. "How well did you know Nathan?"

"We've worked at the camp for the past couple years. He worked with the maintenance crew, and I worked in the cafeteria. Those were our junior and senior years of high school. We're college freshmen now, so we're finally advisors."

"What college do you guys go to?"

"I go to Eastern. He goes to Gonzaga."

"Were you two close?"

Mark shook his head.

"Why not?"

The young man glanced uneasily around before saying, "He's gay. At least, I think so."

"That bothers you?"

"I don't want to be around it."

"Is that why you hit him?"

Mark's eyes widened. "What?"

"He liked guys, so you smacked him. Then you faked it to look like he hung himself."

"No," Mark whispered. His mouth hung open in astonishment.

"Wait. Did he make a pass at you? Is that why you hit him?"

"I didn't hit him at all." Mark's voice rose in panic.

"I'm not sure I can believe that."

"Why?"

"You've already lied about how you found him, so now I think you're lying about killing him."

"He committed suicide. I found him where he was."

"But you lied."

"No, I didn't," Mark whined.

"You're in cabin number three, and Nathan stayed in cabin number four. Right? Cabin number six sits right next to the clearing where Nathan's body was found. If you walked to the cafeteria from your cabin, you would never have passed Nathan's cabin or his body hanging from the tree."

Mark lowered his head, and his tongue darted across his lips.

"At this point, you probably want to start telling the truth."

The young man looked up at Shane. He glanced over his shoulder, then leaned in toward the detective. "If I tell you something, do you promise to keep it confidential?"

"No."

Mark thought for a moment before speaking. "If anyone finds out about this, I'll get kicked out of camp and never be allowed to work the summers again."

Shane's face remained passive.

"I spent the night with Mindy Monahan."

"Where does Mindy stay?"

"Cabin nine."

Shane rubbed his chin and watched the kid.

"It's forbidden for staff to have relationships, especially… well, you know, with another staff member. Anyone found doing it would be immediately excused from the camp. This is a great summer gig, and I don't want to lose it."

Shane thought about telling the kid to control his urges, but an image of Emily popped into his mind. It seemed like the entire department had told him to control his own desires. People in glass houses, Shane thought.

Mark hung his head.

"Mindy can vouch for this?"

The young man's head popped up. "Do you have to ask her?"

"I've got to rule you out as a suspect."

Mark dropped his head again.

Shane stood. "Follow me."

They walked to the parking lot, and Shane waved over Sergeant Lee. "Have this kid sit in your car."

Lee grabbed Mark by the elbow. He escorted the young man to his patrol car and put him in the back seat. When he returned to Shane, Lee looked put out. "I sure as hell hope you're not going to interview each kid one by one. There's got to be twenty-something of them in the cafeteria, and we've got busloads starting to show up."

"I'm the only guy here, Sarge. I'm working as fast as I can."

An older man approached. He wore a brown and green uniform similar to the deputies. He was a senior volunteer Shane had seen around before but had never learned his name. "The lieutenant said you needed someone to watch over a computer or something?"

Shane jerked his head for him to follow, and they headed toward the cafeteria.

Immediately inside the building was a small lounge. Several couches and chairs filled the room. In the corner sat a large wooden desk with a computer and printer. On the opposite side of the room from where they were standing was the door to the cafeteria.

Shane pointed at the computer. "Don't let anyone near that desk."

The older man nodded, "Yes, sir."

The detective then stepped into the cafeteria. Seated in the spacious room were about two dozen teenagers and a couple of adults. Each person had on the white Sunrise T-shirt and khaki shorts that seemed to be the camp uniform. Every head turned his way.

"Mindy Monahan?" he loudly asked.

A young woman raised her hand and slowly stood. She was a thin girl with light brown hair. He waved for her to follow, then he went back outside to the picnic table where he had spoken with Mark. As Mindy walked toward him, she held her arms tightly around her stomach. Embarrassment was evident on her face.

Mindy sat but kept her arms crossed over her body.

"Do you know why I called you out?"

She shook her head.

"Someone killed Nathan Price."

Her face pinched. "I thought he hung himself."

"That's not what happened. Where were you last night and this morning?"

Mindy's eyes widened, and she glanced around. Then, when she spoke, she leaned in and almost whispered, "In my cabin."

"Alone?"

Mindy swallowed hard before nodding.

"You sure?"

She nodded again.

"Why do I get the feeling you're lying?"

Tears welled in her eyes.

"Someone spend the night with you?"

She looked around before nodding.

"Who?"

Mindy blinked several times but didn't answer.

"We're going to sit here until you tell me who you spent the night with."

"Mark," she said. Then whispered, "Mark Brown."

Shane drummed his fingers on the table. "If I report this to Mr. Palmer, you'll both be kicked out of camp, right?"

Her head bobbed as tears flowed down her cheeks. "Please don't tell my parents."

"Do you know of anyone who would want to hurt Nathan?"

Mindy shook her head as the tears continued to flow.

"Did you see anyone using the computer in the cafeteria this morning?"

She wiped the tears away with the back of her hand. "No."

"Did you like Nathan?"

Mindy shrugged. "He wasn't my favorite, but I didn't hate him. He was okay, I guess."

"Did Nathan have any friends?"

"Maybe Tom Baker."

"Tom?"

"They seemed to hang out."

Shane stood. "Stay here," he said and headed toward the parking lot and Sergeant Lee. A green Ford pickup with three ladders in the back pulled into the parking lot, followed by a white van with the star-shaped logo of the Spokane County Sheriff's Office on its side. Forensics had finally arrived.

Lee intercepted Shane, and both men watched the forensics team unload their equipment.

"Sarge, you can use the girl at the picnic bench and the kid in your car to bring snacks and water to the kids on the buses."

Lee's eyes narrowed. "You telling me how to do my job?"

Shane sighed. "I'm telling you that I did mine. Those two are cleared now. I thought they could be of some help to you."

Lee sniffed once. "Fine," he said and walked off toward the forensics team.

Shane headed back to the cafeteria to call out Tom Baker. He was an awkward-looking kid with long floppy hair and a gait that reminded Shane of an old horse. When he sat at the table, he looked like he was ready to pee his pants.

"You're a friend of Nathan Price?"

"Is it true what they've been saying?"

"What's that?"

"That Nathan is dead?"

"Yeah."

His eyes drifted down. "I can't believe it."

"Did he ever say anything to you about being depressed or wanting to hurt himself?"

Tom shook his head. "No. Nathan was a pretty happy guy. He never complained about much and seemed to be happy working up here for the summer."

Shane leaned on the table. "Was Nathan gay?"

Tom glanced over his shoulder and then back to the detective. "Does that matter?"

The detective shrugged. "I'm not sure."

The young man rubbed his face and then ran his fingers through his hair. "He wasn't gay."

"How can you be sure?"

Tom stared at Shane until the detective figured it out.

"Got it."

"I won't admit it because I don't want to lose this job." Tom glanced over his shoulder before continuing. "Being a camp advisor is good money to hang out in the sun for a few months."

"Did Nathan have any enemies?"

"Not that I knew of."

"What cabin do you live in?"

"Number one."

"Okay, Tom. Report to the sergeant over there." Shane pointed to Lee. "He's going to have you get the kids some food and water."

Tom stood and slowly walked away.

Shane pulled out his notebook and plopped it onto the picnic table. He made some quick notes about his conversation with Tom and then stared at his scribblings from earlier.

He flipped a couple of pages back to reread his transcription of the note he found under Nathan Price's pillow.

> *I am sorry for the things I've done. I can never tell you how much hurt I've caused others because of my own perversion. In the past, I've touched boys and for that I'm deeply sorry. I can never be forgiven.*
>
> *- Nathan*

Shane rubbed his chin and continued studying the words.

"Detective McAfee?"

He turned at the sound of his name to see a small woman with light, frizzy hair. Shane recognized her immediately—County Commissioner Janet Carlson. Sergeant Lee hurried across the grassy area toward them.

"Are you Detective McAfee?" she asked.

"Ma'am?"

"I'm deeply concerned at what is going on here."

"Me, too."

When Sergeant Lee arrived, he stood immediately behind the commissioner with a malicious grin on his face.

She said, "Those children on the buses are not prisoners."

"Is your child on one of them?"

"No." She waved away his question. "But I am worried about those children."

"I'm concerned about them as well."

"I don't see how. You're making them stay on those buses."

Shane sighed. He was wasting time with a commissioner who served no purpose in a homicide investigation. "A murder happened here this morning, and I'd like to catch the killer before we let a group of children in."

The commissioner stammered, "Murder? I thought it was a suicide."

"It's not."

Carlson pointed a manicured finger at Shane. "I want to know what led you to that conclusion."

"Ma'am, you're slowing down my investigation."

She looked around, then said, "It looks like you're doing nothing but sitting here."

"That's because I'm talking to you."

Janet Carlson's face pinched. "Detective, I know who you are. Right now, you're a liability to your department because of your personal life. You should thank your lucky stars you're even handling this case."

Shane shrugged. "Ma'am, if you want me off this case, the lieutenant is down that path over there."

Carlson's cheeks reddened before she spun around and bumped into the grinning sergeant. "Where is the lieutenant?"

Lee bowed slightly. "I'll show you the way."

The two of them hurried off.

***

Shane walked around the cafeteria to the administration building. He pulled open the screen door. It creaked loudly as he entered, then banged closed behind him.

An extended counter provided a barrier between the visitors and administrators. A moment later, David Palmer emerged from a back office and walked up to the counter. "Detective?"

"Do you have files on the advisors?"

"Sort of. All the staff, including the cooks and maintenance folks, must pass a background check. I've got the applications they filled out before starting this summer. No one has a file, though."

"Can I see the applications?"

"Sure." Palmer disappeared into his office. A moment later, he returned and handed the detective a stack of papers.

Shane took the applications and slowly flipped through them. "Can I take these with me?"

Palmer shrugged. "I guess so, but I'm not sure if I'm breaking any privacy laws."

Shane ignored his concern and walked back to the cafeteria building. The senior volunteer was sitting on a folding chair near the computer.

"Anybody come by to use the computer?"

The older man shook his head. "No, sir."

Shane sat at the desk. He tapped the keyboard, but nothing happened. He then pressed the power button, and the machine whirred to life. The monitor soon lit up and told Shane the computer had been improperly shut down. The computer ran a diagnostic check before flipping over to the familiar Windows screen.

Shane went to the Start menu and opened the only word processor on the machine—Microsoft Word. It was the same program he used at the department to write his reports. When the program finally opened, a side bar popped up to announce a recovered document that he could view.

He clicked on the unnamed but autosaved document. There on the monitor was the letter Shane had found under Nathan Price's pillow. He stared at the document for a moment.

"Find what you're looking for?" the old man asked.

The detective moved the pointer to the File menu and selected Properties from the available choices. The document's specifics showed it had been created at 7:56 that morning.

Shane made an entry into his notebook before turning to the volunteer. "This is officially part of the crime scene now. No one touches the computer except the forensics team."

The older man smiled as if grateful that his efforts were now necessary.

***

Outside the cafeteria, Shane pulled his cell phone from its holder. Still no service. In his left hand, he carried the applications for the staff. He headed toward the parking lot and saw a large crowd of children surrounding the buses. They appeared restless and anxious to get inside the camp.

Shane walked over to the sergeant's car and climbed in. On the Mobile Data Computer was all the original call information, including who called it in and where the call was from. In the upper right-hand corner, Shane found the time that 911 recorded the call—8:02 a.m.

The letter was created on the computer six minutes before the hanging was reported. There was no way Nathan Price could have returned to his cabin, put the letter under his pillow, and then hung himself. All in six minutes.

Shane now knew without a doubt Nathan Price was murdered, and he could prove it. What he couldn't prove was who did it.

Limited possibilities ran through his mind as he jogged down the path. At the clearing, Lieutenant Reisdorf, Sergeant Lee, and County Commissioner Carlson stood together. Their attention was focused entirely on Nathan Price as four forensic technicians prepared to cut his body down from the tree.

Three ladders were set in a triangle formation, and a technician was at the top of each ladder. The technicians had attached a harness to Nathan. A rope dangled from another branch. A deputy on the ground held the loose rope and prepared for the body's weight to be transferred to him.

Perched on the tree branch, a female technician carefully sawed back and forth across the rope until it snapped free. The deputy held tight to the rope, and Nathan Price's body was carefully guided to the ground by the three technicians.

Commissioner Carlson's face was white. "It's a shame for a boy to take his own life."

Shane coughed once. "It wasn't a suicide."

Lieutenant Reisdorf reached out, grabbed the detective by the arm, and escorted him away from the Commissioner. "What are you doing?"

"My job."

"I mean pissing off the commissioner. She came down here with her panties on fire, wanting me to kick you off the case and suspend you."

"For what?"

"For being Shane McAfee." Reisdorf spat on the ground. "Aw hell," he muttered. "Now I'm spitting at a crime scene. You're driving me nuts, McAfee."

Shane caught the commissioner watching them.

"Why is she here?" Shane asked.

"What do you mean?"

"She told me she didn't have a kid on one of those buses. If that's true, then why is she here?"

Reisdorf turned away from the commissioner so she wouldn't hear his comment. "This is probably going to be high profile, what with it being a camp. She wants the exposure when the camera crews show up. You know how politicians are."

"Have you ever had a commissioner at a crime scene?"

The lieutenant looked back at Carlson. "No."

Shane cocked his head. "Then why is she here?"

The commissioner turned and headed up the path with Sergeant Lee at her side.

"What are those?" Reisdorf pointed at the papers in Shane's hand.

"The staff. It's their applications."

Reisdorf eyed the departing commissioner. "Maybe her kid was never supposed to be on a bus." He patted Shane on the shoulder and left him to get a better look at the body.

Shane quickly flipped through applications to check the names of each advisor. There wasn't a single Carlson in the bunch. Then he turned the stack over. On the back side of each paper was the emergency contact information for each advisor.

Now Shane slowly flipped through the papers. Each advisor had to list two people in case an emergency occurred. About two-thirds of the way through the stack, Shane found what he was looking for. Janet Carlson was the emergency contact for Peter Reynolds. Relation to advisor—mother.

Shane pulled out Peter's form and skimmed through the information. For the last three years, he had been a cafeteria team member for the camp. Before that, when he was in junior high school, he was an attendee at the camp. This year, he would be an advisor.

The detective hurried up the path and continued until he got to the administration building. When the screen door squeaked to announce his presence, David Palmer came out of his office.

"I've been on the phone all morning trying to do damage control," the camp director said. "You can't believe how fast word is traveling."

Shane held up Peter Reynolds's application. "You know this kid?"

Palmer nodded. "Sure. Good kid. Kind of shy, but a hard worker."

"Did he come in and use the phone this morning?"

"Not that I know of, but I wasn't in my office all morning."

"Do you normally leave it unlocked?"

"Sure. Who out there is going to steal something?"

"Did Peter know Nathan?"

"Everybody knows everybody."

"I mean, did they know each other before this year?"

"They've both been at the camp for several years." David looked past Shane and through a window overlooking the parking lot. "Speak of the devil."

Shane turned around and saw Commissioner Carlson walking quickly toward a black Volkswagen. At her side was a young man. "Is that…?"

"Peter Reynolds. The one and only."

Shane dropped the papers on the counter and ran out of the office. The screen door banged loudly behind him.

Janet Carlson and Peter Reynolds glanced back at the noise.

"Stop!" Shane yelled.

"Get in the car, Peter!" Janet barked at her son.

Peter opened his car door and climbed in.

Shane sprinted across the parking lot. His vision tunneled on the commissioner and her son. He didn't see Sergeant Lee racing toward him. Shane was almost to the Volkswagen when Lee reached out and grabbed his arm. Shane spun and crashed to the ground. Pieces of gravel tore into his hands. He scrambled back to his feet, ready to jump at the sergeant.

The commissioner climbed into her car and shut the door.

"The hell do you think you're doing?" Shane yelled at Lee.

"You were going to attack her."

The two men stood behind the commissioner's car, blocking it from leaving.

Shane pointed at the car. "She's taking her kid from an active crime scene. That's interfering with an investigation."

Lee shook his head. "He didn't do anything."

"How do you know?"

"I asked him." The sergeant crossed his arms over his chest.

"You talked to the kid?"

"He said he didn't see anything or do anything."

"Then why in the hell is she rushing him out of here?"

Lee shrugged but kept his arms crossed. "She wants to take him home."

Shane threw his hands up in the air. "No shit, she wants to take him home!"

"I don't see the problem."

"The problem is, he had to have called her this morning after the body was found. Otherwise, how else would she know to rush out here?"

Lee looked at the boy in the car. "He didn't do it."

Shane pointed at the car. "Get the kid out of the car so I can talk to him."

"I'm a sergeant in this department, and you better show me some goddamned respect."

"How about I ask the lieutenant to get the kid out of the car…" Shane's voice trailed off.

Lee glared at Shane for a moment before dropping his arms and walking to the driver's door. He tapped on the glass, and Janet Carlson lowered the window. "I'm sorry, ma'am, but Peter needs to talk with Detective McAfee."

The commissioner opened her car door and stepped out. "I'm not letting my son talk to that misogynistic bastard. You already asked Peter your questions, and you said you believed him."

Lee bowed his head slightly. "It's not my investigation, ma'am."

"Who is the sergeant here?"

"It doesn't matter," Lee said, his voice soft.

"Get the sheriff down here. I want to talk with him."

"Yes, ma'am," the sergeant muttered.

"Commissioner," Shane said, calling her attention to him. "Did your son play any role in the murder of Nathan Price?"

"No," she snapped. Then she shook her head and lowered her voice. "No. Of course not."

"Then let me ask him a couple questions. After that, you can take him home."

Janet Carlson's face reddened, and her jaw muscles tightened, but she said nothing.

"Ma'am," Shane said. "We can still have the sheriff come down, but I don't think we should delay this any longer. All those kids are waiting for camp to start."

Carlson glanced toward the buses and the children. Shane imagined her counting the number of voting parents. "I stand by Peter when you ask your questions."

"That's fine."

Janet Carlson bent down to the car. "Peter, please talk with the detective."

The young man climbed out and stared at Shane. He stood about five-foot-eight with a bad case of acne. Peter glanced at the camp buildings. When he looked back at Shane, his eyes squinted.

The detective moved toward Peter, and the young man took a step back.

"What are—"

The kid turned and ran.

"Hey!" Shane yelled as he tore after him.

"Peter!" Janet Carlson screamed.

"Stop!" Sergeant Lee hollered.

Peter had the advantage of youth and quickness, but Shane's stride was longer, and every few steps, he got a little closer. They raced toward the end of the administration building before Peter pulled up, easing into a trot.

Shane tackled him, and they rolled down the slight hill past the edge of the administration building and into a small clearing near the maintenance shed.

Peter struggled against Shane's grasp as the detective tried to put a pair of handcuffs on his wrists. "I didn't do it," Peter yelled.

Shane clicked the handcuffs into place and rolled the young man onto his back. "Then why'd you run?"

"I didn't know if they could see us."

"Who is they?"

Sergeant Lee sprinted up to Shane. "You okay?"

"Yeah. He's not—"

"I was talking to the kid," the sergeant said.

Shane looked back at Lee to comment, but the sergeant had already grabbed his shoulder microphone. "We got the kid. Everyone return to their positions."

The detective asked the young man, "Who were you worried about seeing us?"

Peter jerked his head toward the maintenance shed.

Shane looked at the small structure. "Is someone in there?"

"I dunno, but those are the guys you should start talking to."

"If you're worried about them seeing us, why did you run toward it?"

Peter shrugged. "I don't know. I've never run from the cops before."

Shane stood with his eyes fixed on the shed. "Watch him," he said to Lee and headed toward the small building. Shane pulled his gun out of its holster and let it hang by his leg.

The maintenance shed was about twenty feet by thirty feet. The sides were painted barn red, and the metal roof was painted white. A thick padlock on the front door stopped Shane from getting in. He tugged on it a couple of times, hoping it would pop open. When it didn't, he walked around the shed and found no windows to peek through. From the corner of the roof, a small wind chime hung and tinkled lightly in the breeze.

Next to the building was a gravel area with a sign that read, Maintenance Crew parking only. In the middle of the gravel was a shiny white van with Sunrise Camp for Boys and Girls printed on it.

Shane studied the building a minute more before walking back to Peter. He slipped his gun back into its holster as he walked. Janet Carlson ran up to her son and stood in front of him, blocking Shane. "How dare you hurt my child!"

"Get out of the way." Shane reached past her toward Peter.

Carlson slapped Shane's arm.

The detective immediately jerked his hand back. He stepped closer to the commissioner. "I could arrest you right now for assault. Either let me finish with your son, or that's exactly what I'll do."

Sergeant Lee carefully reached out for the commissioner. "Ma'am, you need to let the detective finish."

Carlson let herself be pulled away, but she kept her eyes firmly on Shane.

The detective reached down and lifted Peter to his feet. "What's with the maintenance shed?"

Peter looked around before saying in a hushed voice, "There are two types of kids who do maintenance work at the camp. Some do it until they get to be an advisor. Those kids always get the grass mowing and landscaping jobs. Then there are those kids who connect with Albert, the maintenance supervisor, and those kids turn strange."

"Strange? What do you mean?"

"They don't hang out with the rest of us anymore. They do their job, and that's it. Sometimes, during the summer, they come and go as they please for days at a time. Normal kids can't do that. Not even the advisors can leave like that."

Shane remembered Price's file. "Nathan used to work on the crew."

Peter nodded. "But he wasn't one of the strange ones."

"Why wouldn't you tell me this in the parking lot?"

"Nathan and I talked last night after dinner. He thought he saw something but wouldn't tell me what it was. He didn't want to freak me out if it was nothing."

"Did he hint at what it was?"

"Nathan said it dealt with Albert, and now he's dead. I don't know what's going on, but I don't want to be next."

"Who's on the maintenance crew?"

Peter gave him a list of names, explaining who worked the grounds and who was part of Albert's special crew. When he was done, Shane released Peter to his mother and went back to work. As the detective walked away, he could hear the commissioner complaining to Sergeant Lee.

"I want his badge," she said. "I want that man out of the department."

***

The screen door to the administration building squawked as Shane yanked it open. When he stepped inside, he paused at the counter and heard David Palmer hurriedly say, "I gotta go." A moment later, the camp director appeared in the doorway of his office.

"Detective?"

Shane walked around the counter, past the director, and into the back room.

Palmer protested. "What are you doing?"

Shane sat on a wooden chair in front of the director's desk. Palmer slowly walked around and sat in his own chair. Shane noted that a walkie-talkie had been placed on top of a stack of papers in the middle of the desk.

"Detective, are you all right?"

Shane ran his fingers through his hair. "Who is Albert?"

Palmer tilted his head. "What?"

"Albert? Who is he?"

"He's responsible for the maintenance of the campgrounds."

"Is he here all year round?"

"Yes."

"Does anyone else stay here all year?"

"No one."

"What about you?"

"Besides me," Palmer said, his voice suddenly small.

"Only you and Albert are here all year long?"

Palmer nodded.

Shane studied the black telephone on Palmer's desk. "Who were you talking to when I walked in?"

"Who was I talking to?"

Shane smiled. Repeating questions was often a sign of stalling or lying. He leaned forward in his chair. "Who were you talking to?"

"A concerned parent."

"Which one?"

"Uh, Ruth Erickson. Chuckie's mother."

Shane nodded. "Can I use the phone for a second?"

Palmer smiled and said, "Yes, of course."

Shane slid the phone over and lifted the receiver. It was cool in his hand. Shane's finger hovered above the redial button for a moment before he hung up the phone.

"You weren't on the phone."

"What?"

Shane grabbed the walkie-talkie. It was warm in his grip. "This is the first walkie-talkie I've seen since getting here. One unit by itself is worthless. It takes two to make a conversation. Who's on the other unit?"

Palmer's face went slack, and he stared into Shane's eyes. Then, he muttered, "I didn't kill Nathan."

"Who has the other unit?"

"Albert," David said.

"Albert who?"

"Albert Martin."

Shane clicked his tongue against his teeth. "Where can I find Albert?"

"I can't tell you."

The detective jumped to his feet. "Where is Albert?"

Palmer closed his eyes and shook his head.

Shane's voice rose in anger. "Did Albert kill Nathan?"

The camp director continued to shake his head, but now his hands were at his temples.

"Did Albert kill Nathan?"

Palmer opened his eyes as tears streamed down his face. His mouth fell open, but no answer came.

With his free hand, Shane slapped the desk. "Damn it, Palmer!" he yelled. "Did Albert kill Nathan?"

"Yes," the camp director said, "Oh, God, yes."

Shane set the walkie-talkie back on the desk. It crackled to life. "I'm going to kill you, David," a low, menacing voice said.

Palmer's eyes widened. "You… you had the radio on?"

Shane leaned over the desk. "Now tell me where Albert is hiding before he gets to you."

Palmer wiped the tears from his face with the palms of his hands. "There's a storage shed near cabin eleven. He's in there."

The detective grabbed the walkie-talkie and ran out of the administration building. The door slammed closed behind him.

***

Shane sprinted to Sergeant Lee, who stood near his patrol car. A smirk creased his face. "Commissioner Carlson is gonna have your—"

"Get on the radio," Shane said.

"I don't take—"

"Get some deputies to the storage shed near cabin eleven. Price's killer is hiding out there."

Lee straightened as he took in the gravity of Shane's words.

"His name's Albert Martin." Shane backpedaled from the sergeant. "Also, go to the admin building and watch Palmer. He's part of this."

The detective spun then and sprinted toward the path with the walkie-talkie still in his hand. His feet propelled him along the narrow, twisting way. Step after step, his heart pounded harder.

When Shane's right foot landed awkwardly on a rock, his ankle twisted, and he tumbled to the ground. He dropped the walkie-talkie as he fell. The skin on his hands, already torn from the earlier fall in the gravel, ripped open further. He snatched the radio, scrambled to his feet, and continued up the path. His ankle howled with pain.

He raced past the clearing and the forensic team as they were bagging Price's body. Lieutenant Reisdorf stared dumbfounded as Shane sprinted by.

All the detective heard was the lieutenant say, "What the—"

At cabin eleven, Shane climbed the steps, two at a time. When he reached the top, he found three deputies, sweat on their faces and their guns drawn. "Behind the cabin," Shane rasped as he struggled to control his breathing. "The storage unit."

The lead deputy shook his head. "There ain't no storage unit here."

Shane took the words in but still sprinted behind the cabin. He spun around, looking for anything resembling a manufactured structure, but there was nothing. The deputy came up next to him.

"Shit," the detective muttered.

"You want us to fan out? Maybe look deeper in the woods?"

Shane shook his head. Amid gasps of air, he said, "The camp director would know exactly where a storage unit was. He sent me on a wild goose chase. Call Sergeant Lee and have him hold the camp director until I get back there."

The detective bent over and struggled to regulate his breathing. He listened as the deputy tried to reach Sergeant Lee on the police radio. After the third attempt, the deputy said, "He's not answering."

"Get someone there. Now!"

Shane sprinted down the steps. His legs strained as he raced, and his right ankle tightened. Sweat burned his eyes as he darted past the clearing where the lieutenant still watched over the forensic team.

His stomach ached as he climbed the path toward the administration building. A yank of the screen door, and he was inside. Lying behind the counter was Sergeant Irvin Lee. He moaned as he sat up.

Shane hopped over him and ran into the office of the camp director. It was empty. He went back to the sergeant. "What happened?"

"I don't know." He bent forward to rest his head between his legs. "I only turned my back on Palmer for a second."

Shane leaned against the counter. He keyed the walkie-talkie he had taken from Palmer and lifted it to his mouth. "Albert, where are you?"

There was no answer.

"Albert, this is Detective McAfee. I need to talk with you."

The radio was silent.

"David, if you're with Albert, you're just as guilty of killing Nathan."

The radio crackled to life. A soft noise tinkled before a voice said, "Go to hell."

The tinkling noise was familiar, and Shane struggled to place it. He stepped outside and looked around. The kids from the buses were milling about the parking lot. He could hear them talking excitedly among themselves, and many were staring at him. With concern on their faces, Mark Brown and Mindy Monahan moved toward him.

An engine fired up, and Shane looked over his shoulder, down the length of the administration building. Then he remembered the tinkling sound from the wind chime hanging at the edge of the maintenance shed.

The nose of the maintenance van turned the corner and pointed right at him. The berm was to his right. The admin building and the cafeteria were to his left. The only way out for the van was through Shane and into the parking lot, which roughly two hundred children now inhabited.

The detective turned toward the kids. "Get back!" he hollered at the advisors. "Get them back!"

Shane spun around as the van lurched forward with its engine roaring. In a single motion, the detective dropped the walkie-talkie and drew his gun. He squeezed the trigger repeatedly, and the gun bounced in his hand. The children behind him screamed.

The van swerved several times before colliding with the admin building, tearing off chunks of wooden siding. Shane jumped out of the way, his feet and hands propelling him up the side of the berm.

The van freed itself from the building but swung wildly to the left and up the small grassy hill. It bottomed out and stopped suddenly a few feet in front of Shane.

The detective stood and moved toward the van. His gun led the way. David Palmer was in the passenger seat, a deflating air bag in front of him. Shane pulled open the door and reached out to press two fingers against Palmer's neck. He was breathing but unconscious.

Shane stepped up the berm and around the van's front to see Albert Martin at the wheel. He moved to the door and opened it. Albert was unconscious. The air bag from the steering wheel was still shrinking.

Albert was a big man, fat around the midsection. A heavy red beard covered his face, and a thick batch of red hair covered his large head.

Shane turned slightly to press the fingers of his left hand against Albert's neck. A pulse throbbed under Shane's fingers.

Albert's eyes popped open, and he jerked toward Shane. The detective jumped, and the ground gave out beneath him. Shane fired his gun into the air as he fell backward, down the berm. His shoulders hit the ground before he rolled head over heels and landed on his hands and knees.

When Shane shook his head to clear it, he realized he had dropped his gun. Albert was out of the van now and moving toward him. He clutched a knife in his right hand. The detective pushed himself up and leaped to the side as Albert wildly swung the blade.

Then the heavy man turned and lowered his head like a bull preparing to charge. Shane saw his gun a few feet away and dove for it. He scooped it up as Albert ran at him. The detective fired once, and the bullet hit Albert in the throat.

The big man stopped, dropped his knife, and clutched his neck with both hands. Blood flowed through his fingers.

Albert's eyes emptied as he looked at Shane. When he took a step toward the detective, Shane pulled the trigger again. Unfortunately, he hadn't realized the slide had already locked back. His gun was now empty.

Shane prepared for an attack that never came. Albert took a stuttering step forward before falling to his knees. For a moment, he stared at Shane with lifeless eyes, then pitched face-first into the ground.

***

Thirty minutes later, Shane was seated on the picnic bench in the grassy area.

David Palmer sat across from him with his hands cuffed behind his back. He cried softly to himself.

"Albert's dead," the detective said.

Palmer nodded.

"Why did you kill Nathan?"

"Not me. Albert."

Shane sipped some water. "Fine. Why did Albert kill Nathan?"

"He was afraid Nathan would tell the cops."

"What did Nathan discover?"

Palmer laid it out for Shane, breaking into tears and sobs as he went along. Finally, when he was done, he rested his forehead on the table.

"Final question. Why didn't you type Nathan's suicide note in your office?"

"I didn't know Albert had killed Nathan. I found out about it when Mark reported it to me."

"So, Albert typed the note?"

"I didn't do it."

Shane waved over a deputy. "Take him and book him for murder."

Palmer objected, but Shane ignored his protests. He walked over to where the lieutenant stood.

"Did he say why they killed the kid?"

Shane nodded. "It seems the camp was a middle point for a smuggling ring running contraband in and out of Canada."

"You don't mean marijuana?"

"No, but they were running other drugs and people without documents."

"People? You mean illegals? Maybe terrorists?"

Shane shrugged. "We'll need to look more into that. He was sort of vague. Point is, they were into illegal trafficking, and the kid stumbled onto it. Martin and Palmer couldn't let that info get out, so they took care of the kid."

"Were both of them in on the killing?"

"Palmer denies helping, but he covered it up, so he's just as guilty."

The lieutenant scratched his cheek as he thought. "Why were they doing that crap here, at a summer camp?"

"For that reason, exactly. The two of them lived here year-round. They could move dope or people or whatever else they wanted. What cop is going to pay much attention to a summer camp van?"

"I guess that makes sense."

Shane stood and watched three news vans pull into the parking lot. The group of kids huddled in the far corner of the parking lot still waited for the camp to be opened. With their microphones extended, the various news crews hustled over to stand in front of the children.

"Good luck," the detective said and clapped his hand on the lieutenant's shoulder.

Shane McAfee walked down the path toward the clearing where Nathan Price had been found. He stopped and stared up at the branch from which the kid had hung. His own recollections of summer camp were light and airy. Two hundred kids would now be cheated of those memories.

The detective turned and stared at the afternoon sun shimmering off the water. Hunger ached in his belly, but he knew there were several more hours to be spent out here. His investigation had turned into an officer-involved shooting. That meant more detectives were on the way from the Spokane Police Department. They would take over the scene and soon interview him.

The roles would reverse, and he would be questioned. But he had done nothing wrong, so he had nothing to fear.

He shoved his hands in his pockets and frowned. Sadness overwhelmed him.

Maybe he should break it off with Emily, he thought. Be responsible and listen to the concerns of the others in the department. Avoid the political blowback that comes with seeing a mayor's daughter, especially one so many years his junior.

He glanced up again to the branch where Nathan Price had hung. He then thought about the blood that gushed through the fingers clutched around Albert Martin's neck. Both men started the day alive and probably never imagined they would die before sunset.

"No," he said to himself. "There's no way I'm breaking it off. No matter who says what."

Shane McAfee turned and walked back toward the cafeteria to wait for the detectives to arrive from Spokane. Then he would go home, crawl back into bed, and forget about the whole damn day.

The Greatest Show on Earth

"I don't wanna die!"

Blood flowed through his fingers. A red ring grew around the neck of his white Independent T-shirt. He writhed on the ground, screaming in panic. His unshaven face was pale, and his eyes drowned in fear. When he looked up and saw me standing over him, he shrieked once more.

"I don't wanna die!"

***

Minutes before, I casually chatted with an attractive woman many years younger than me. She was in her mid-twenties, with large doe eyes and a fresh face.

"Busy tonight?" she asked.

"Not so bad."

An espresso machine loudly hissed as it worked. I was next to a twenty-four-hour drive-thru coffee shop. Due to its all-night nature, I'm sure the barista got more than her fair share of men making googly eyes at her. I tried not to be one of those creepy guys, but she wore a half-shirt that exposed her flat belly. Her bare stomach was at eye level, which meant I had to look at it every time I turned toward her.

"Well, it's still early." She frothed the milk for my latte. "Things will pick up. They always do, right?"

"Once the bars close—"

"Oh, my God." She faced me with a disbelieving expression. "Bar customers are the worst. Am I right?

They come here to get a coffee—like that's going to
sober them up."

"The same thing happens at the Jack in the Box. That
place is a mess after the bars close."

The barista smirked. "If I didn't need this job—"

"Tell me about it."

She had a belly ring—a little silver one—that I
couldn't help but stare at. I felt like a fish attracted to a
shiny thing. Do they know not to bite the hook but are
compelled to do it, anyway?

I pulled my attention away from the shiny loop when a
dispatcher called for several units. After he shared the
location of an incident, the operator dispatched several
officers. Leaving my microphone in its dashboard hook, I
pressed the transmit button.

"Lima Thirty-six," I said.

"*Thirty-six*," the dispatcher responded. "*Go ahead.*"

"I'm only a few blocks away. Put me on that call."

The barista eyed me. "Leaving so soon?"

"Gotta run. Will you hold that for me?"

"Oh, I'll keep it warm for you, Sarge." She winked.

It was too much flirtatiousness from a woman her age.

I pulled away from the coffee stand, then activated the
emergency lights and siren. With a spin of my steering
wheel, I accelerated into the roadway.

***

A large crowd huddled together in front of the skate
park. Several scurried away at the sight of a law
enforcement vehicle entering the area. The remaining
group parted to expose a body lying on the sidewalk.

I pulled to the nearest curb and parked.

As I approached, those in the thinning crowd muttered taunts of "five-oh" and "bacon." None of them were more openly aggressive than that.

A white male writhed on the sidewalk. Blood covered his ghost-white skin. He wore dirty fatigue pants and torn-up Converse. "I don't wanna die," he screamed wetly, clutching his throat with both hands. Dark blood seeped through his fingers.

I keyed my mike. "Lima Thirty-six. I'm with a conscious white male, early twenties. He has a severe laceration to the neck. Start medics."

The radio squawked before the dispatcher announced, *"Thirty-six, copy. Be advised Fire is already en route."*

The skate park was located under the freeway and had initially appealed to the area's youth. Now, it attracted drug users, the homeless, and other general malcontents. It was a mecca for trouble, and it smelled like trash, urine, and feces.

I leaned over the young man and loudly spoke above his screams. "I'm Sergeant Marino."

He screamed in reply.

If the paramedics hadn't been notified, I might have pulled the first-aid kid out of my trunk. But it was too early in the night for the fire boys to be safely tucked away in their beds, and I didn't feel like getting covered in blood.

"I don't wanna die!" he shrieked in a desperate gurgle.

I asked his name, but before he could reply, a couple of patrol units barreled into the area, running code. Lights bounced off the nearby buildings, giving the night a disco effect. The officers jumped out of their cars and trotted over.

Karen Bradshaw got to me first. She was in her early thirties and a damn good patrol officer. I asked her to locate witnesses. She nodded and waded off into the crowd.

The other officer was a civil service poster child—twenty years on the job and thirty extra pounds around the waist. He wouldn't do more work than asked, and any reports he wrote would be terrible. I gave him the best job for his talents.

"Tape off the scene. Give me fifty feet both ways. We've got a first-degree assault and are going to need to lock it down."

As usual, he glared at me for giving him an order, but that look faded when he realized how little actual work he'd have to do.

I turned back to the young man on the ground. He had a swastika tattoo on the inside of his right forearm, and a smell of feces emanated from him. "What's your name?"

He cried out in a mix of pain and fear.

When he didn't answer my question, I said, "I need your name before the medics get here."

The idea of help seemed to reach him. "D—D—Dustin," he stammered. Tears rolled down the sides of his face.

I pulled my notebook from my pocket and continued my questions. "Last name?"

"Jones," he said and quickly followed it up with another piercing shriek. I was thankful the kid had an easy-to-understand name.

When the fire department arrived, the engine's roar and its siren's whine covered the kid's screams. Four burly firemen hopped from the rig and double-timed it over. They squatted and immediately set to work. One of the medics commented to another that the kid had lost a lot of blood. I took that as a bad sign and moved in while they worked.

"Who did this to you, Dustin?"

He shrieked.

I leaned over. "Dustin, I need to know who did this."

He averted his gaze. "Guys."

"What guys?"

"Dunno!" he weakly screamed with his eyes closed.

One of the firemen working on the kid glowered at me.

"Why'd they do this to you?" I asked.

"Dunno." He mumbled. "Dunno."

I crossed my arms and frowned. He was lying.

If Dustin wouldn't share what happened, he was no longer a victim in my book; he was part of the problem. I would still need to figure out who did this to him and why—that was the job. However, the crusader part of my psyche—the part that wanted to right wrongs and rescue people—would take a backseat to the clerk portion—the part of me that simply dotted i's and crossed t's. Reports needed to be completed with all the appropriate boxes checked so a detective could take over. But paperwork did not require emotional involvement.

If Dustin Jones wasn't concerned about justice for himself, then why should I worry?

A medic pulled Dustin's hand away from his neck. Blood freely poured. "It's coming fast," the fireman called out. "The carotid's been clipped."

Another medic cut open the kid's shirt to check for other wounds.

Someone walked up from behind and touched my elbow. I glanced over my shoulder to see Karen, then turned my attention back to Dustin. She spoke into my ear while we watched the firemen work.

"One of the kids in the skate park said his girlfriend did this. Said they argued, she pulled out a quote big-ass knife unquote and stabbed our boy in the neck. When he hit the ground, she walked off."

"Just like that?"

"That's what the witness said. Girl walked off like she didn't have a care in the world."

"Did you get a description and direction?"

"Of course."

I glanced back, and Karen rolled her eyes.

"Not my first rodeo, Sarge."

"Nice work. Broadcast the girl's description, then see if you can find another witness."

Karen patted my shoulder before leaving.

I called dispatch. "Lima Thirty-six."

"Thirty-six, go ahead."

"Send a couple units down here. We need to secure the scene for a first-degree assault investigation."

The medics continued to work as sirens from an ambulance grew closer. One firefighter used his hands to hold Dustin's head steady.

I leaned over. "Dustin."

He focused on me.

"Why'd your girlfriend stab you?"

His eyes widened, and he tried to scream, but it came out as a weak warble.

"When I find her, I'm going to charge her with a felony. You understand that, right?"

"My fault," he muttered. He sounded as if he were falling asleep. "All my fault."

Several of the firemen glared openly at me now.

Screw them, I thought. Let them feel put out. They'd go back to their comfortable fire station after this, maybe make some chili, sit their fat asses in a recliner, and play some video games. We were the ones who had to clean up the messes out here.

When the ambulance pulled on scene, the firemen cleared the way for the EMTs. While they strapped the kid onto a gurney, I jotted entries into my notebook about what I observed at the scene. The details were needed for my report. So I looked up once more to take it in.

There was blood everywhere, and people of all ages stood as close to us as possible. Their wide eyes filled with excitement and wonder. Welcome one and all to the greatest show on earth, step right up, and gaze upon the wonder of city life.

After the medics loaded Dustin, I climbed into the ambulance. My presence would be for the possibility of a dying declaration—something that I could later attest to in a court of law—not because I worried about the kid. It was simply another box to check while building a case against the girlfriend. Would I have felt different riding with a citizen—someone we pulled from a neighborhood with a name like South Hill or Five Mile? Maybe, but citizens often played the same games with us that Dustin did. Getting emotionally involved with their problems was the quickest way to an ulcer, a breakdown, or an early exit from the career.

The vehicle rocked from side to side as we sped toward the hospital. Dustin's skin appeared whiter than before, and his eyes took on a distant stare.

Over the hum of the ambulance, I asked, "Why'd she stab you?"

He didn't answer. Instead, he only cried weakly. His early screams had stopped.

The EMT next to me hurriedly made notes on a clipboard.

"Dustin," I said.

His voice was so soft I had to lean in.

"I broke up with her."

"Why do that?"

"I wanted—" He closed his eyes.

"Why'd you lie?"

"Because—" His face twisted in pain.

The EMT shouted to the driver, "He's fading! Call it in."

Dustin stared up through his fog of fear and whispered, "She loved me."

***

When the ambulance jerked to a stop, the EMT yelled, "Out!"

I jumped from the rig. The medics removed the gurney and were in the hospital so fast that it reminded me of a NASCAR pit crew at Talladega.

I pulled the radio from my hip and called Karen. "Lima Thirty-six to David four-twelve. Status check."

"Four-twelve," she responded. *"We've located the suspect. She's in custody, and I'm en route to jail. I'll contact you on the way."*

Inside the hospital, several staff members sprinted into a room already crowded with EMTs and doctors. I leaned against a nearby wall and watched them work at a level that could only be described as controlled madness. Minutes passed before the work abruptly stopped. They wandered out, one by one, each with their head down.

When a nurse walked by, I asked for the time of death.

"Twenty-three thirty-four," she muttered. By the way she took the loss, she was either new or would burn out in a few years from over-caring.

I pulled out my cell phone and called the department's on-shift lieutenant. He needed to be notified that the crime was no longer an assault. He would then alert the on-call detectives to respond to the scene of what was now a homicide.

***

As I walked out of the hospital, a patrol car pulled up to the front. A young woman sat in the backseat behind the thick plastic shield.

Karen Bradshaw slid out of the driver's seat and put her hand on top of the car. "This is Heather Watson."

The teenager in the back had dirty dreadlocks. She also wore the same type of fatigues as Dustin.

"What'd she tell you?"

"Nothing."

"Clammed up?"

Karen nodded. "I read her Miranda, and she said she understood them. But that was it. She never said anything beyond her name and birthday."

We watched Heather for a moment, but the girl stared impassively straight ahead. If she knew we were studying her, she either didn't care or controlled herself exceptionally well.

I opened the back door of the patrol car. "Heather, I'm Sergeant Marino."

She didn't face me.

"Why'd you stab Dustin?"

No reaction.

"He said you stabbed him because you loved him."

Still no reaction.

"I thought that was a crazy thing to do for love, but what the hell do I know?"

Heather faked a yawn.

"I'll give you this, sister. You've got good aim."

Her gaze flicked to me, then casually returned forward.

"He's dead."

She twisted her lips before uttering, "So?"

"That's what you want in our report? *So?*"

Heather stared straight ahead and didn't answer my question.

I closed the door and turned to Karen.

She softly asked, "The kid died?"

"A few minutes ago. I've already notified the lieutenant. Major Crimes will be out in a bit."

"Well, I better get the prom queen home before she turns into a pumpkin." Karen blew out an exaggerated sigh before climbing into the driver's seat of her patrol car. She pulled away, then turned north, heading towards the jail.

In the dark of a warm summer night, I watched her departing taillights. Then I wondered if the barista with the belly ring still had my latte.

Dwight's Girl

The smell of cooking hamburger pulled Dwight Murphy slowly from his nap. When his eyes fluttered open, he sat upright in the old La-Z-Boy recliner. A rerun of *Seinfeld* played quietly on the television. He must have fallen asleep during the episode of *The Big Bang Theory*. It was the last thing he remembered.

The multicolored lights on the nearby Christmas tree blinked rhythmically. Outside, snow fell in the night sky.

In the small kitchen, Marlene cooked dinner. She wore a blue turtleneck and faded blue jeans.

The aroma of dinner teased Dwight's nose, and he scooched to the edge of his chair. "Smells good."

She shrugged. "It's Hamburger Helper."

"Sounds good, too."

Marlene chuckled. "A few more minutes, and it'll be ready."

Dwight watched his wife move around the kitchen. She was a tall, thin woman whose long hair fell below her shoulders. She was ten years younger than him. Being with her made him feel like the luckiest man in the world. "Excited for Christmas?"

Marlene stirred the concoction in the frying pan. "Two more days."

"I can't wait for that ham."

She glanced up. "Is that the only reason you're excited?"

It would be their first Christmas together. He had never spent the holiday with anyone but his mother, and she died fourteen years prior.

A smile pushed at the corners of Dwight's lips. "It's not the only thing."

"It's not?"

"I'm looking forward to pumpkin pie as well."

Marlene laughed. "Well, in case you want to know, I'm looking forward to spending it with you."

Dwight climbed out of his chair and walked over. He slid his arms around her waist and kissed her gently on the neck. "I love you."

She leaned back and kissed the side of his face. "I love you, too, but you're going to make me burn dinner. Go sit down."

Dwight playfully patted his wife on the rear and returned to his chair. Marlene caught him watching her, and a pleased smile spread across her lips. He winked once before laying his head on the recliner's headrest and closing his eyes.

A sharp knock on the front door caused Dwight's eyes to snap open. He started to climb out of the chair, but Marlene made a disapproving sound.

"I'll get it." She wiped her hands with a dishtowel. "Take it easy. You had the hard day at work today, not me."

He dropped his head back to the recliner.

***

It only took Marlene a few steps to get to the front door of their one-bedroom apartment. She pulled the door open and inhaled reflexively.

In the doorway stood a large black man. Snow covered the shoulders of his puffy black jacket. "Hey, baby."

Marlene frantically shook her head.

He looked past her into the apartment. "Been some time."

She brought her hand up and covered her mouth.

"You left without saying goodbye. I've worried about you. Non-stop."

"Whozzit?" Dwight called from the living room.

"I got arrested," he continued, "and you disappeared." He snapped his fingers. "Like that. Just disappeared. Do you know how that can make a man feel?"

She had difficulty swallowing now. "How— How did—"

"How did I find you?"

Marlene nodded.

"Lots of people remember you. You're hard to forget. One of them saw you walk into this building—like a citizen. I couldn't believe it, so I had to see it for myself." His eyes traveled up and down her length. "You look good, Rhonda. Healthy even."

Tears welled in her eyes at the mention of her old name.

"I thought you left the city, but you're still here. Why wouldn't you have left? I figure that means you wanted me to come and find you. Am I wrong?"

"Please, Junior," Marlene whispered, "please go."

"Honey?" Dwight stepped around the corner.

***

Dwight cocked his head to hear better the conversation between his wife and the man she had just called Junior. Marlene stiffened when he touched her back. "Honey?"

121

"Well, well, well," Junior said with a widening grin. "Another rooster in the henhouse. This is why you haven't come back."

Dwight appraised the size of the large man at his door. He was several inches taller and maybe fifty pounds heavier. "Can I help you?"

"How are you going to help me?"

A confused smile crossed Dwight's face. "What is it you want?"

The man motioned toward his wife. "Rhonda."

Marlene tensed further.

Dwight's brow furrowed. "Who's Rhonda?"

Marlene glanced over her shoulder. Tears streaked her mascara.

"Marlene?"

"You told him your real name?" the visitor asked. "You must like this one."

She sobbed and covered her face with her hands.

Dwight leaned in. "Honey, what's going on?"

Through her fingers, Marlene said, "I'm sorry. I'm sorry."

Dwight's pulse quickened, and he pulled her back from the door. He stepped in between her and the visitor. He puffed his chest with pride and bravery he rarely felt. "It's time you go."

He swung the door, but Junior slapped it, stopping it from closing. The bigger man stepped into the apartment.

"You can't come in here," Dwight said.

The bigger man smirked. "I can go wherever I—"

Dwight shoved Junior in the chest.

This act of defiance seemed to surprise the bigger man. He barely moved, though, just bent his back as if being blown by a stiff wind. Junior slapped the side of Dwight's face.

Stumbling backward, Dwight fell into Marlene, and they both crashed to the floor. He tried to get up, but Junior placed a foot on his chest.

"Stay there, chubby, or you'll get hurt."

Dwight thought about fighting, but Junior wasn't attacking him now. Instead, the man concentrated on his wife.

Marlene stared helplessly up at the visitor. Her eyes were wide, and the little sobs now accompanied the tears.

"Time for you to come home, Rhonda." He reached out for Marlene.

"This is her home," Dwight said weakly. "She's my wife."

Junior glanced at him before raising an eyebrow at Marlene. "That true?"

She shook her head until Dwight cried, "Marlene!"

The sobs grew, and she nodded.

"Well, shit," Junior muttered and pulled his hand back. He then took his foot off Dwight's chest. "Now, look what you've done, Rhonda. This is going to require some negotiation."

She covered her face, and her shoulders bobbed in rhythm to her weeping.

"Get up," Junior said in a frustrated tone.

Dwight hurried to his feet and backpedaled into the living room.

Junior grabbed Marlene by the arm, lifted her, and led her deeper into the small apartment.

"Sit," he ordered, and both Marlene and Dwight dropped onto opposite ends of the couch.

The big man walked into the kitchen and turned off the stove. He lifted a spoon and inspected the dinner Marlene had been preparing. "I can't believe you eat this." He tossed the spoon into the sink.

"What's this about?" Dwight asked. The weakness in his voice didn't surprise him. He was not built for confrontation. He'd only been in two fights his entire life—once in grade school, the other in middle. He'd lost both badly.

"What's this about?" Junior said mockingly. "Tell him, baby."

The way the visitor called his wife "baby" worried Dwight.

Marlene lowered her head and wailed.

"Tell him, Rhonda," Junior demanded. "Oh, that's right. Tell him, Marlene."

Dwight looked at his wife. "What's going on?"

She lifted her gaze to him. "I— I worked for him."

His eyes flicked to Junior. "Doing what?"

Marlene did not answer her husband.

Junior stepped forward. "Tell him, *Marlene*, or I will. Probably best if it comes from you."

She muttered something, but it was too soft for Dwight to hear.

"What?"

"He was my pimp."

"That means—"

"C'mon, man." Junior dropped into Dwight's recliner. "She fucked for money."

Marlene stared straight ahead.

"No," Dwight said. His eyes locked onto his wife. "I don't believe it."

Junior shrugged. "Believe it, or don't. Doesn't make any difference to me, but that's what she did. A lot of it, too."

Dwight turned his attention to the man sitting in his chair.

"She never told you, huh? Can't say as I'm surprised. I'll say this. She was the best I had—no lie. A straight earner. Just delicious with what she could do. Guys would come from out of town for her."

Dwight's jaw muscles tensed.

"She had a habit that she needed to feed. That's what brought us together. Remember that, baby?" Junior pulled a little leather pouch from his pocket and shook it.

Dwight noticed how Marlene's eyes snapped to it.

"You see that, chubby? That's the monster right there."

Marlene closed her eyes and looked away.

"Fight the good fight, girl." Junior chuckled. "You got yourself clean, then found a new man. How long you two been married?"

When she didn't answer, Dwight croaked through dry lips, "Three months."

The pimp shook his head. "I should charge you for that, but you didn't know she was giving away product for free. I'll make her put some extra hours in. Then we'll be square."

With a sudden flash of courage, Dwight jumped to his feet. "You can't do that!" His fists balled and hung at his sides.

Junior's speed surprised him. The big man leaped out of the recliner and was on top of Dwight in the blink of an eye. The two men collapsed onto the couch.

Dwight swung helplessly at Junior. His fists bounced off the big man's shoulders. Junior punched him several times in the body then headbutted Dwight, which removed all fight from the smaller man.

Marlene screamed, and the visitor backhanded her.

Junior slowly climbed off the couch and surveyed the damage he'd caused. "Well, chubby, chubby, still think I can't collect what's mine?"

Dwight protected his head with his arms and balled up on the couch. Marlene reached out to touch him but stopped when Junior spoke.

"Touch him, and I'll beat you just the same."

She pulled her hand back, then hugged herself.

The big man glanced at the Christmas tree and flicked a silver ornament with a finger. His eyes drifted to the few presents underneath the tree. "Pathetic." Junior returned his attention to Dwight. "Sit up."

He struggled upright while the bigger man returned to the recliner.

The three of them sat quietly for a few moments. Eventually, Junior said, "Rhonda was special."

Marlene stared at the floor.

"Want to know what she used to do?"

"No."

Junior ignored his refusal. "She worked a stroll. Know what that is?"

Dwight closed his eyes at the words.

"Yeah, you know. You ever hire a girl before?"

Dwight shook his head.

"For real? You seem the type. Anyway, Rhonda also did a bunch of flicks for some South Hill pervs. The stuff they were into, you wouldn't believe."

Dwight opened his eyes, and Junior pantomimed a camera. Marlene hugged herself while rocking back and forth.

"She went through a lot of men during her time. How many do you think she handled? I never really thought about it before, but I bet we could get a rough estimate."

Dwight rubbed his left eye and tried to ignore the throbbing in his head.

"I like easy math," the pimp said, "so let's say she worked three hundred days a year. We both know she worked more, but round numbers are easier to do in my head. Sound fair?"

Dwight stopped rubbing his eye and glared at Junior.

"Some nights, she struck out, but there were others where she turned four. So, let's average two a night."

He winced.

"That's six hundred a year." Junior paused and scratched the stubble on his face. "That seems light, don't it? Real light. Maybe I underestimated. Maybe I should have averaged three. No, some of them guys were repeat customers—the good ones, anyway. You sure you never paid for it?"

Dwight's stomach roiled.

"But still six hundred tricks a year. Not bad mileage."

Marlene ran into the bedroom and slammed the door behind her.

A deep laugh grew from within Junior. "Ready to give her back?"

Dwight stared ahead and pressed his lips tightly together.

"She lied, man. Your whole marriage is a sham. She probably even convinced you that you were the only man for her—maybe even her first."

Dwight hung his head. Marlene hadn't said he was the first, but the only one for her? Yeah, she had said something like that.

"Don't feel bad, chubby. Hundreds of guys have felt that way. Hell, she made me believe it every time we were together. Girl has a way. That's why she's special."

Dwight squeezed his eyes closed.

"When you're done, kick her ass out. She knows where to find me, and I can always use her talents." The big man stood. "Guess I should get goin' and let you two lovebirds get on with the rest of your holiday."

Junior headed toward the front door. On the way, he stopped outside the closed bedroom door. He lightly tapped. "Rhonda, baby, you know where to find me."

When he was alone, Dwight stared at the blinking lights on the Christmas tree. He had never believed in God, but now he fully accepted the existence of the devil.

***

An hour later, Marlene left the bedroom, strode into the bathroom, and closed the door. Dwight heard the lock turn.

The shower kicked on, and twenty minutes later, the water shut off. Marlene shuffled back into the bedroom and closed the door behind her. Again, he heard the lock turn.

Dwight never moved from his spot where he watched the blinking Christmas lights. His mind overflowed with the horrible images Junior had described.

He fought to reconcile his feelings.

When Marlene opened the bedroom door, she padded slowly into the living room. She wore a pair of black pajama bottoms and a black T-shirt with a "Zip's Hamburgers" logo above her left breast. Her long, wet hair was pulled back, and her face was free from make-up.

She knelt in front of Dwight and wiped away the tears that streaked his cheeks. "I'm sorry that I didn't tell you."

Sobs grew from his chest.

"That's not who I am anymore. I don't use, and I don't trick." Marlene touched Dwight's knee.

He frowned. "Those meetings you go to—"

"The narcotics ones?"

"I thought—" Dwight didn't finish his statement because he didn't know what he thought. Marlene went to meetings several times a week, but he never wanted to pry into her past, and she never felt the need to divulge why she went. She only said she had a problem. He realized he'd been too trusting. He always thought she was too good for him.

But now he knew the truth.

"I love you," she said. When he didn't answer, she continued. "I didn't think you could accept what I had done before. I never meant to hurt you, but I couldn't risk losing you. I couldn't change my past, so that's why I hid it."

Amid his sobs, Dwight sucked for air.

"Please, understand," she continued. "I would do anything for you—*anything*."

He looked down at a stranger he once thought of as his wife.

Marlene wiped more tears from his face. "Talk to me, Dwight. You're scaring me."

His lip trembled.

"Please," Marlene pleaded. "Say something. Say anything."

Dwight's hand whipped out but stopped short of hitting his wife. She flinched and now stared at her husband with fear.

"You made me a fool."

Marlene shook her head. "No. I didn't. I wouldn't."

"I bet other men have done things to you that you've never let me."

"Dwight—"

"I guess I didn't have enough money."

Marlene slapped him, and he slapped her back. Then he slapped her once more, this time harder. She collapsed to the floor.

"Whore," he muttered. He stood above her. "Dirty fucking whore."

Dwight walked over to the Christmas tree and yanked the string of lights from the outlet. The room darkened.

Marlene scrambled to her knees and reached out for him. "Dwight, please—"

He smacked her hands away. "Don't you ever touch me—*Rhonda*."

Dwight stormed by her and into the bedroom. He grabbed his gym bag and hurriedly stuffed it full of clothes.

In the living room, Marlene wept.

When he finished packing, Dwight slung the bag over his shoulder and stalked out of the apartment, angrily slamming the door behind him.

***

For some time, Marlene simply lay on the carpet and curled up in a ball. Her body trembled as she cried. It shook as the weeping grew deeper with despair.

When the tears stopped, a calmness entered. Memories of dulled pain oozed into her veins and wormed their way through her body. She sat upright and put her back against the recliner. She wiped her runny nose with the back of her hand.

Outside the apartment, a group of carolers sang. Their voices drifted into the apartment.

"Oh, come all ye faithful…"

The darkened Christmas tree and unopened presents mocked her. She kicked a colorful box near her foot and sent it skittering across the carpet. It came to a rest near the wall, unchanged.

"…joyful and triumphant…"

Remember the Rifleman

It took Lowell Stuckart a moment to realize there was music.

He lay there, staring into the darkness, trying to determine why he'd awakened until a nearby *boom-boom-boom* caused him to sit up in bed.

It was typical for passing cars to have their music too loud, but it was often temporary, as the annoying intrusions would quickly fade into the distance. This noise didn't diminish, however. The *boom-boom-boom* of a heavy bass line repeated.

Lowell swung his feet off the bed and stood. He shuffled toward the light switch but stopped with his finger hovering above it, thinking better of turning it on.

Instead, he grabbed the shotgun resting against the dresser and stepped into the hallway. Cradling the weapon, he moved toward the other bedroom—the one that overlooked the front of his property and the street. As he entered the room, the music stopped, and he froze.

In the sudden silence, he heard an engine running. At least, he thought he heard a motor. After a couple of seconds, he shook his head. It must have been his imagination. He bent over and crept toward the edge of the window. He pushed the curtain to the side and peeked out.

It hadn't been his imagination.

The road was almost seventy-five feet from the house. A stone wall, three feet tall, ran the length of his property. Various trees and bushes stood behind it. At the mouth of the driveway, a car was backed in with its brake lights illuminated. Underneath the full moon, the vehicle appeared black, but it could have been any dark color.

A spotlight near the driver's door slowly moved over the thick batch of trees that lined the property on the other side of the street. That small forest separated him from the rest of downtown Spokane.

Lowell's nearest neighbors were a hundred yards in either direction. Trees, bushes, and elevation changes kept them from seeing one another.

The spotlight moved slowly across the lower level of the trees in a determined search pattern.

Lowell sighed and relaxed. The shotgun dangled in his right hand.

He was awake now, and he wouldn't have an easy time getting back to bed. Sleep was often elusive for him. He trundled back to his bedroom and returned the shotgun to its resting place against the dresser.

Then he walked down the stairs to the kitchen, still leaving the lights off, to make a cup of tea. He opened the microwave door, activating its interior light to illuminate the nearby counter. He searched for a flavor of tea and selected his usual—Earl Grey. Why he even bothered to look at the others was a mystery.

After he heated the water in the microwave and added a teabag, he poured a splash of milk into the cup. Lowell then sat near the living room window so he could watch the police car in his driveway. The thought of walking out and talking to the officer never crossed his mind.

Years ago, a citizen had approached a sheriff's deputy while the lawman was writing a report. The deputy was parked on the citizen's property. There was some confusion about what occurred next, but the result was not in dispute. The citizen was shot and killed.

Therefore, Lowell stayed safely in his chair. He let his mind drift about who the officer outside was searching for and what that person might have done. He imagined that the officer was part of a larger perimeter, and therefore other officers must be in the area. The forest was too large for one man to search alone. Also, whoever they were looking for must be considered a severe threat to spend this much time searching for him. As Lowell sipped his tea, he estimated more than fifteen minutes had gone by since he first got out of bed.

His mind soon tired of the act of wondering, and his thoughts drifted to his son and daughter-in-law. They lived on the other side of the state in Olympia. It had been almost six months since he'd last seen them and several weeks since he'd spoken with his son. Lowell thought he should probably call in the morning and check on them.

The police car's searchlight continued its slow scan of the forest as Lowell again sipped from his tea.

Next, he considered the various chores he had waiting at his rental properties. He needed to blow out the sprinklers, a leaky sink required fixing, and if he had time, he would purchase some deicer and snow shovels. Winter would be here soon enough, and he needed to prepare the tenants.

Lowell now put the empty cup aside and struggled not to nod off. The tea was working, and weariness crept back into his body. But, as usual, when that happened, his thoughts turned to his wife, Sophia. It had been almost ten years since she was taken to be with her Lord.

Over forty minutes passed before the police officer finally switched off his spotlight, activated his emergency lights, and sped away from the mouth of the driveway. Lowell put the teacup in the dishwasher and went to bed.

The clock showed 2:27 a.m.

As he started to fall asleep, a thought slowly worked at the edges of his brain until it pushed front and center.

Did the police find who they were looking for?

Or did they give up?

***

An hour after he climbed from bed for the second time, a shadowy figure emerged from the woods.

Lowell was now seated in the second-floor bedroom, the one with the view to the front of his property. The figure ran from the woods and crossed the street. The shadow darted into his driveway and hid against the nearest tree. It stayed there for some time.

Lowell assumed it was a man due to the size. He didn't bother to think his inference was sexist. A man of his generation wasn't bothered by such things, especially when a stranger was hiding in his yard.

He had just started to count the passage of seconds when the figure ran toward the house. Lowell backed from the window, raised the shotgun to his shoulder, and waited to hear some sort of entry. When the noise didn't come, he moved to the back bedroom and peered through the wooden blinds toward the garage. The darkened figure was looking for a way into that structure.

For a moment, Lowell considered calling the police. This thought vanished, though, when the figure skulked toward the house.

Lowell moved to the top of the stairs. He strained to hear if the man had entered the house. Not hearing anything, Lowell began to walk down. When he heard the unmistakable squeak of the kitchen door opening, he stopped.

Had the figure heard him and stopped, too?

Lowell's heart thumped inside his chest, and his hands were sweaty around the shotgun. He crouched now and listened, straining for any telltale sounds.

The figure entered the living room and slowly moved toward the stairs.

Lowell flicked the lights on then and pointed the shotgun at the intruder.

The man wore a black beanie, a black jacket, and black pants. He immediately lifted his gloved hands in surrender.

***

The early morning sun had not peeked above the horizon yet, but already the sky had a purplish hue. Several police cars were in Lowell Stuckart's driveway, and uniformed officers milled about the house's exterior.

Lowell sat at his kitchen table, smoking a cigarette. Spokane Police Officer Adrian Thorn and Detective Jim Morgan sat with him. The two men were in plain clothes. Morgan was a thick-chested man who wore a leather coat and a tightly curled baseball cap. His face carried a particular cruelty. Thorn was several years younger, with long hair. He wore a denim jacket with a hooded sweatshirt underneath. Both men had silver badges dangling around their necks. Only Thorn had a notebook out.

The detective's gaze remained keenly focused on Lowell as the officer explained that the two men were part of a specialty unit within the department. They had been tracking a fugitive who had fled into the woods.

"Homicide detectives are on the way," Thorn said, "but I'd like to ask you some questions,"

Lowell inhaled on his cigarette. "Shouldn't I wait to talk with them? They're going to ask me the same questions."

Thorn leaned back and glanced at Morgan.

The detective said, "Talk to whoever you like, but you did us a favor. We'd like to know how it went down, seeing as we chased this guy for a week."

Lowell considered his words, then shrugged.

The officer lifted his pen. "You told the responding officer that you saw a patrol car in your driveway."

Lowell inhaled again on his cigarette. "After it woke me with its loud music, yes."

"What happened after that?"

"When the officer left, I went back to bed, but I couldn't sleep. So, I watched a show."

"Where?" the detective interrupted.

Lowell thumbed toward an older box set on a wheeled cart.

"I take it you weren't streaming it."

"Streaming?"

"From the internet."

"I don't have the internet," Lowell muttered. "I don't want the government spying on me."

The detective nodded. "Understood." He checked his watch. "What were you watching?"

"*The Rifleman.*"

Morgan's brow furrowed, and he slowly glanced toward the television. "I remember that show." When he turned back to Lowell, he continued. "My grandfather liked it. We used to watch it together when I was a kid. One of the few nice memories I have of the man."

Lowell's eyes narrowed. "They don't make actors like Chuck Connors anymore, do they?"

Morgan motioned for the officer to continue, but his gaze returned to the old television set.

Thorn asked, "What happened after?"

"The show?" Lowell said. "I got tired and turned off the television. I grabbed the shotgun—"

"You normally keep a shotgun with you?"

"When I get spooked, yeah, and that other officer did a good job of doing that with his loud music and parking in my driveway."

Thorn crossed his arms and studied Lowell. "You don't like us much, do you?"

"I like you fine."

"Not me," the officer said. "Cops. Something in the way you talked about the other officer. I get the feeling you don't like us much."

Morgan's gaze returned to Lowell.

The older man eyed both officers before shrugging. It seemed the best course of action when dealing with cops.

"Why is that?" Thorn asked.

Lowell flicked the ash from his cigarette. Another shrug wouldn't do now. So he said her name. "Sophia."

"Who's that?"

"You still haven't found her killer."

"I'm not sure I know what you're—"

Morgan tapped the officer's arm. "Sophia's his wife."

Thorn cocked his head.

The detective nodded. "I've been here before. Back when I was on patrol."

Lowell took another drag on his cigarette and studied the detective. Morgan didn't look familiar, but it was years ago, and if the man was in a uniform, well, it was a bad night. Lowell didn't remember much from that day.

Morgan continued. "I was first on scene. The call was a nine-one-one hang-up." To Lowell, he said, "You were out of town, right? Some conference back east."

"Philadelphia."

"A suspect broke into their home," Morgan told Thorn. "He was still here when his wife returned. At least, that's what the investigators surmised."

Lowell remained still as the detective studied him.

"Your wife called for help, but someone yanked the cord from the wall. By the time we arrived, it was too late."

Officer Thorn glanced back and forth between the detective and Lowell. Then he said, "If this was some sort of revenge, Mr. Stuckart—"

"I already told you," Lowell said. "He had a knife."

"That he took from your kitchen."

"Yes."

"How did he get in?" the officer asked. "There was no forced entry. Was the kitchen door unlocked?"

Lowell shrugged. "I must have forgotten to lock it."

"Forgotten?"

"It happens."

"After your wife was murdered?"

Lowell's face warmed.

"Did you order him to stop?" Thorn asked. "Or to get out?"

"He had a knife, and he was inside my house." Lowell worried that his response might have been too forceful, but the officer was irritating him. Why didn't they believe him?

Thorn shook his head. "It doesn't fit."

Lowell flexed his jaw as his anger at the officer bubbled under the surface.

"This guy," Thorn continued, "the one you shot, was never violent. Never. He was a burglar. Mostly broke into commercial buildings and stole things. He escaped from our custody. We had him because he was going to help us catch someone worse—much worse—than him."

Lowell flicked his cigarette again, even though there was no ash to knock free.

"This guy didn't even hurt anyone when he escaped. He just ran. That's what he did whenever he faced arrest. The uniforms were tracking him with the dog when they had to call it off because of a drive-by shooting across town."

"What are you saying?"

"What I'm trying to figure out," the officer absently tapped his notepad, "is why he grabbed a knife?"

"I wasn't inside his head, so I don't know."

"Neither do I." Thorn glanced at Morgan. "Do you?"

The detective shrugged.

Thorn continued. "And since he's dead, we'll never know, will we?"

Lowell inhaled on his cigarette, then pointed with it to the officer. "You know what I do know? He was in my home—*illegally*—with a knife. It's the same type of weapon used on my wife. I wasn't taking any chances since you guys failed to catch him earlier."

"Him?" Thorn asked. "Which him are you referring to? Our burglar or your wife's murderer?"

Morgan leaned over to the officer and whispered, "Adrian, we're good."

Thorn eyed the detective. "The hell?" he whispered.

"Head back to the station and write it up."

Thorn snapped his notebook closed. "Something stinks."

Morgan watched the officer stalk away. When it was just the two of them, the detective calmly turned to Lowell. "You blasted him. Cold-blooded."

Lowell froze.

"You know it, and I know it. If you believe in God, he knows it. Hell, even Thorn knows it."

Lowell opened his mouth, but the detective held up his hand. "Don't say anything. Just listen."

The two men watched each other for a moment before the detective continued.

"Thorn is good police, and he's going to go back to the department, and he's going to start writing his report. And he's going to come across a piece of information that he'll fact check. I'm sure of it because that's what he does. Then he'll turn over that nugget to whichever homicide detective catches this case."

Lowell blinked a couple of times but remained silent.

"I only know of one channel that was showing *The Rifleman* recently. I know that because I've stopped on it a couple of times. And that channel quit showing it two weeks ago."

Lowell glanced over his shoulder at the television.

"Now, you could have been watching it on a streaming service, but you already said you don't do that. And by the age of your TV, I'm going to guess you don't have a DVR. Know what that is?"

Lowell's chin dropped to his chest.

"Maybe you've got it on DVD, or maybe you got a VHS tape, for that matter. Whatever you've got, that's what you meant when you said you watched it on the television. Is that what you meant?"

Lowell's eyes lifted.

"But by that look, I'm going to guess it's not."

The cigarette in Lowell's fingers burned him, and he jumped. He snuffed it out in the ashtray.

Morgan stood. "Mr. Stuckart, I'm sorry that we didn't find the guy who killed your wife. I wish we had. She didn't deserve to die like that."

"Maybe it was this guy."

"This guy was a turd, no doubt, but he wasn't the one who killed Sophia. This guy would have robbed you blind, but he would never have hurt you."

Lowell gently rubbed the fingers that were burned.

"The homicide detective is going to be here soon. Better get your story straight. Figure out how you watched *The Rifleman*."

He tried to swallow, but his mouth suddenly felt dry.

Morgan asked, "Got a computer?"

"Yeah."

"Maybe say you watched it on YouTube instead and were confused if Thorn calls you out on it. Claim PTSD with the shooting and all."

Lowell's brow furrowed. "I've never been on YouTube. I wouldn't have the faintest idea where to start."

The detective shook his head. "How's that my problem? You're the one who remembered *The Rifleman*. Not me."

Lowell's eyes narrowed. "Why are you telling me all this?"

Morgan shrugged. "What am I telling you? We're not even talking. We never even had this discussion."

"But I—"

"But let me ask you this. Killing this guy didn't bring your wife back, did it?"

Lowell stared at him.

"Revenge never works out the way we plan."

"This wasn't about revenge," Lowell whispered. Even to him, it didn't sound believable.

"Better work on that," Morgan said. "Right now, you sound guilty as hell."

The detective walked away without looking back.

The Serious Business
of Ira Hammerstein

On July 17, Ira Hammerstein woke several minutes before six a.m. He lay in the darkness of the bedroom, listening to his wife, Rachael, snoring softly next to him.

After a while, Ira reached over and turned off the alarm clock that was set to sound promptly at six. He sat up, swung his legs off the bed, and slipped his feet into a pair of leather slippers. Then he stood, straightened his pajama top, and repositioned the bottoms. Once adjusted, Ira shuffled quietly from the bedroom into the kitchen.

He started a pot of coffee brewing before retrieving the newspaper from the front porch. Ira returned to the kitchen, sat at the table, and began reading the paper as he did every morning. His eyes scanned several stories before he sighed and shook his head. The news of the day no longer held any relevance for him. He carefully folded the paper and placed it at the front door for Rachael to take with her to work.

He wandered into the reading room, just off the stairway, and selected a collection of Mark Twain short stories. Ira returned to the kitchen, poured a cup of coffee, and sat to read his favorite short story, "The Notorious Jumping Frog of Calaveras County."

Shortly after seven a.m., Rachael walked into the kitchen. She was wearing a brown pantsuit with a large brooch over her left breast. Her short, brown hair was perfectly coiffed, and her make-up was, as always, neatly applied. At forty-two, Rachael was still the most beautiful woman Ira had ever seen.

Rachael poured herself a cup of coffee before turning to her husband. "Already done with the paper?"

Ira nodded. He had finished reading his favorite Twain tale and was now absently flipping through the remainder of the book, looking for familiar passages that might make him smile.

"Not going into the office today?"

"No, I think I'm going to call in sick. Take a mental health day, so to speak."

Rachael studied Ira. He hadn't missed a day of work in five years. The last absence was due to passing a kidney stone. Nevertheless, Ira loved his job as an auditing supervisor for one of the largest accounting firms in Spokane. "Do you feel all right?"

"Sure." He sipped from his cup.

"Okay," she said with a bit of a shrug.

Rachael walked over to Ira and leaned in to kiss him goodbye, her lips stopping a millimeter before touching the skin of his forehead. She made a smooching sound and stepped back.

"Have a good day," she said and left the kitchen. Her perfume hung in the air for several minutes after the front door closed.

When Ira finished his coffee, he put the cup in the dishwasher and returned the short story collection to the reading room.

Ira detoured to the bathroom and took a leisurely shower. He dressed in a pair of black slacks, black loafers, and a white polo shirt.

Once he was dressed, Ira entered his study and removed four large envelopes from the bottom drawer of his desk. Three of them had been sealed and addressed the day before. The fourth envelope, while full and sealed, was not addressed.

Ira took the three addressed envelopes and left the house. He mailed them at the nearest post office with return receipts requested. He was careful to keep his proof of mailings, as well as the receipt for the charges.

When he returned home, Ira gathered up the unaddressed envelope, a pad of paper, a roll of Scotch tape, and a pen. He sat at the kitchen table and wrote a three-page letter.

When the letter was complete, Ira returned the notepad, tape, and pen to his office. From the closet, he pulled out the Colt M1911 that his grandfather had carried in the Korean War. Ira had cleaned the pistol several times each year following trips to the gun range.

Ira pondered the religious implications of what he was about to do. He was born Jewish but had converted to Christianity twenty years ago to woo and marry Rachael. Both faiths were now distant memories to him, but he was sure his soul would be condemned if it had not been already.

Ira walked into the bathroom, climbed into the bathtub, and closed the shower curtain. He put the gun to his temple, asked his oft-forgotten God for forgiveness, and pulled the trigger.

***

When Rachael returned home from work shortly after six that evening, she immediately sensed something was wrong. There was a strange smell she couldn't place, and a feeling of dread pressed in on her.

On the kitchen table was an oversized envelope and a folded letter. Written on both items were the words "Read before calling emergency services."

Rachael froze as these words sank in. She backed away from the table, turned, and hurriedly searched the house.

She found Ira in the bathtub. At the discovery, she screamed. She sobbed as she rushed back to the kitchen to call 911.

She lifted the telephone receiver and heard the dial tone. Then she saw the envelope and letter again as her finger hovered over the number pad. She put the receiver back and returned to the kitchen table.

Rachael opened the letter and began reading.

> *My dearest Rachael,*
>
> *I have always loved you and must admit I still love you. You were my first love and have remained my only love.*
> *My only wish is that I could have been that for you.*

Rachael stopped and reread the last sentence.

> *My only wish is that I could have been that for you.*

Her mouth went dry. She pulled out a chair and sat at the table.

> *I know about you and Henry Ralston. I discovered your infidelity by accident, as I had always trusted you. I found a repeated*

number on your cell phone bill that you were calling late each night after I had long gone to bed. It only took a little ingenuity and the Internet to discover who that phone number belonged to.

I am sorry to confess this, but I hired a private investigator to follow you the past two months. I had to know for sure because my suspicions were eating away at me.

Rachael lifted her hand and covered her mouth.

The pictures that were taken of you and Henry were not flattering and were damaging to me in ways you would not understand.

Even with the pain and embarrassment you caused me, I couldn't confront you. You always chided me for not fighting for the things I wanted at my job, but you always allowed me to back down from you in our relationship. Maybe that is why you started seeing Henry. Perhaps it was my being twelve years your senior. Or maybe it was something else.

Regardless, I wanted to confront you, but I didn't have the courage. I couldn't stand the idea of accusing you of this and truly losing you forever to Henry.

Instead of facing you directly, I talked with Ronald about my discovery.

Rachael whispered, "Oh, no," through her hand. Ronald was Ira's oldest and dearest friend. He was also the owner of West Land's Construction Company and Rachael's boss. She was employed as the company's bookkeeper.

> *It did not surprise him to learn of your infidelity. He suspected as much but was hesitant to bring it to my attention. Upon my revelation to him, he asked me to audit all his accounts. He had begun to suspect money was missing, and he believed you to be responsible. He hadn't mentioned it before because of our friendship but did admit he was close to challenging you about his suspicions.*
>
> *After some considerable research, I found what you were trying desperately to hide from both Ronald and me. I didn't reveal my findings to Ronald because I wanted to find where you had hidden the money.*
> *With the help of the private investigator, I finally found your account at the credit union. The $20,000 is still there. I did not attempt to remove it.*
> *You may or may not have found my body by now. I could not have faced you with all of this, so I took what some may consider the easy way out.*

Bile rose in Rachael's throat, and she ran to the sink to vomit. She shook for several minutes as she struggled to regain her composure. Once she felt strong enough to continue reading the letter, Rachael returned to the table.

In the envelope are copies of your cell phone bills, your credit union account statement, the photographs of your infidelity, and the general ledger showing how you stole money from our friend. I've included a detailed summary of how I found all this information and how it proves your guilt.

Rachael tore open the envelope, and its contents spilled out. She shuffled items around until she knew that Ira was indeed telling the awful truth.

I have sent a copy of all these materials to Ronald, the police department, and the newspaper. The first two are obvious in their intent. The packet to the newspaper is to guarantee the story gets out. Your father's friendships won't be any protection from the police department as long as the newspaper is watching.

Taped to the last page of this letter are the post office receipt and the proof of mailings to confirm this to you.

You can call the police now and report my death. I am sure, however, that they will have more questions for you tomorrow.

Rachael cried as she looked at the evidence Ira had accumulated against her. She knew her life was ruined unless she figured a way out before calling the police to report Ira's death. She picked up the phone and called Henry. She told him about the letter, the evidence, and how copies of everything had been sent to the police and the newspaper.

"You're on your own," Henry said.

"What?" Rachael asked, not believing what she'd just heard.

"I didn't steal that money. You did."

"But you encouraged me to do it."

There was a pause before Henry said slowly, "That will be tough to prove in court."

"You bastard! I need your help."

"Like I said, you're on your own."

With that, the phone went silent.

Rachael cried for another hour as she tried to think of a way out. In the end, she went to the bathroom and retrieved a short bottle from the medicine cabinet.

She looked at the body of her husband in the bathtub. "Why, Ira?" she asked. "Why?"

Rachael returned to the kitchen and filled a glass with water. It took a while to swallow all the pills in the bottle.

She lay on the living room couch and cried herself to sleep.

***

On July 18, an envelope arrived at the West Land's Construction Company. Another was delivered to the Spokane Police Department. A third arrived at the newspaper office. None had a return address. No one was identified as the envelope's recipient.

The mail clerk at each location opened the envelopes to discover whom to direct the correspondence.

Each discovered the same thing inside the envelopes.

Thirty pages of blank paper.

Marlene

The little man slapped her across the mouth and sniggered when she fought to get free.

It wasn't the first time Marlene Anderson had ever been struck. It wasn't even the first time she'd been hit during sex. However, the previous times it occurred, she was told before it happened, and she was adequately compensated for it.

However, this strike was unexpected, and the little man delighted in her attempts to get out from under him.

"Goddamn it, Felix," Marlene hollered. "Get off."

Felix Stegall giggled and slapped her again. This time was harder, and he held his hand up as if ready to backhand her.

Clawing his chest failed to do anything except further excite the man. He brought his knuckles across her cheek and squealed with glee.

With panic rising in her, Marlene bucked and twisted, shoved, and hit. Felix laughed openly now and punched her directly in the face.

Afraid of another strike, Marlene covered her head with her arms, but Felix suddenly stopped hitting her. Instead, he became deathly quiet, and he stiffened. His features contorted, and he squeaked in the weird high-pitched way that Marlene had heard before.

She shoved him then. "Get off."

He moved from the bed to the corner of the room, where he hurriedly yanked his condom off. Unceremoniously, he dropped it to the motel floor.

Marlene sat upright on the bed and touched her face with her fingers. When she saw the blood, she muttered, "Son of a bitch."

Felix didn't make eye contact as he hurriedly dressed.

"Hitting is gonna cost you double."

He dropped onto the chair to tie his shoes. "I already paid fair market."

Marlene jumped from the bed and stood naked before him. Her feet were spread shoulder-width apart, and her fists were balled. Blood ran from her nose, and her eyes were wild. "Pay me, or I'll scream bloody hell. You know what happens then."

Felix stopped tugging on his laces. His eyes widened, and he swallowed with some difficulty.

"That's right," Marlene said. "That black bastard will come in here and make you wish you never laid a hand on me."

"Let's not get hasty."

"Double!"

He stood and dug his wallet out of his back pocket. He tugged several bills from the billfold, and Marlene snatched them from his hand.

"Never again," she said. "You know better."

"I'm sorry. I got excited. Next time, I'll pay double up front."

"No. Not again. You're not worth it."

"Triple. I'll pay triple."

She sighed and closed her eyes. "Triple. *Up front*."

"Thank you." He tried to kiss her on the cheek, but she pulled back. "Yeah, yeah," he muttered. "Too soon. I get it." He grabbed his suit jacket and slipped by her. After he left, the door closed automatically behind him.

Marlene sat on the edge of the bed and stared into the mirror above the dresser. Her long hair was twisted, black tracks of mascara ran from her eyes, and blood leaked from her nose down over her lip.

She smeared the blood with her fingers, then studied the rest of her body. Her once attractive figure had been ravaged by the hard years and harder drugs. Her breasts had shrunk, her belly had softened, and her skin hadn't had a healthy glow since she left high school. Even though she wasn't even thirty yet, she looked ten years older than that. If she could cry, she would. Instead, she hung her head and sighed.

The door to the motel opened, and a thick-chested black man strolled in. He wore a black leather jacket that fell to his knees. A gold ring glittered on his right hand.

A step behind Junior was his new girl—a young blonde woman with short hair and twitchy eyes. She wore black shorts, a black sports bra, and black sandals—the clothing contrasted with her alabaster skin. Marlene imagined Junior pumping away on Amber, and the vision soured her stomach.

Not long ago, she had been Junior's bottom—his number one. That was before the life took its toll on her, and she broke. Then she ran away and got married. Life was supposed to be different after that, but Junior found her and exposed the awful truth to her new husband.

Junior leaned in and studied Marlene. "The hell happened to you, Rhonda?"

He used the street name she'd carried for many years—the one she refused to readopt after he pulled her back into the game.

"He hit me."

The man's eyes narrowed. "Why didn't you holler? I'd have made that mother—"

Marlene held up the cash. "I charged him double."

Junior slipped the money from her hand and shoved it into his jacket pocket. "That's my girl," he cooed.

Marlene's pulse involuntarily quickened at the words. "Next time, he'll pay triple."

"Triple? You already negotiated an increase?"

"Seemed the best time to do it."

Junior smiled and rubbed the back of her neck. "Good girl. Really good."

The simple touch made her feel like things might be okay. It was stupid, though. Marlene knew she was being manipulated. That was the rational part of her brain talking. She hated that part. It was the part that made her feel bad.

Junior patted her now. "You got the room all day, and there's another cat outside waiting his turn."

Marlene bowed her head. "Can I get a taste?"

"After this one, I'll hook you up. You'll coast through the rest of the day. I promise. But this one you gotta do straight."

"Straight?"

"He's paying for a girl to be clean. He doesn't want one that's junked up."

Marlene doubted it was the john who cared if she was high. More likely, it was Junior training her to be his again. But she understood the rules. That was the rational side of her brain at work—the side she hated at times like this.

She stood naked in front of him and Amber. The other woman curled her lip in disgust.

"Clean up your face," Junior said. "I don't want nobody claiming you're not the best product in the city."

He grabbed Amber's wrist and led her away.

Marlene walked into the bathroom.

***

That night Marlene sat on the old, threadbare couch in her little apartment and stared absently into the distance. A cracked television leaned in the corner of the room. It hadn't worked since she threw a frying pan during a drunken rage. Dirty dishes were stacked on the kitchen counter and the smell of rotting food hung in the air.

Memories of the man she considered her true father flooded back to her. Several times, he had tried to rescue her from this life. He died a couple of months ago. She had never gotten to see him again.

What would her life have been like if she left with him the last time he came back?

What would it have been like if she left with him the first time he showed up?

Images of her husband drifted into her thoughts. Dwight loved her for an idolized version of who she was. She presented the best of herself to the man. That's what she did when she was paid, so why not do it for someone she loved? However, Dwight left her when he found out about her past. Junior shared her shameful secret right before Christmas. Dwight walked out and never came back. That was six months ago.

What would her life have been like if she told him the truth up front?

What would it have been like if Junior never showed up that day?

Would she still be living a lie?

In the apartment next door, a headboard slammed against the wall. It had happened before, and Marlene knew what it was. Amber lived there.

They lived next door to each other in the Moorehouse apartments. Junior put the younger woman there because he wanted Marlene to keep an eye on her—to help her acclimate to the life. He said Marlene would be her mentor, and Amber would be the apprentice. They were stupid words, she thought.

But Junior was always trying things like that—using ideas and concepts to twist the girls up and get them to work together or fight amongst themselves. She didn't understand his logic for keeping them in constant turmoil, but she was smart enough to know that's what he was doing.

Since no girl ever brought home a trick to their apartment, the banging next door could only mean one thing—*Junior*.

He visited all the girls to keep them in line. It was stupid to think she was any more special than the others. However, it wasn't too long ago that she was.

Marlene curled in a ball on her couch and cried.

***

The following day Marlene awoke and sat upright. Her head hurt, and her mouth was dry. She shuffled into the kitchen and ran some tap water into a glass. Her stomach turned when she took a sip. She hurried into the bathroom and threw up.

That day Junior set her up with five johns.

The first three were traditional types—missionary men, she referred to them. Lay down, get it done, and leave.

The fourth made her pleasure herself while he took photographs. He made odd little noises every time he snapped a picture. She fought hard to keep the disgust from her face.

The fifth one broke her in a way she no longer thought possible. She froze in surprise when she opened the door.

"Hello, Rhonda," Dwight said, using the name he'd only spoken once in anger. He walked by her and into the room.

"What are you doing here?"

He pushed down on the mattress, feeling its springiness. "This is where it happens, huh?"

"Dwight?"

He unbuttoned his shirt. "I'd ask if you missed me, but it's been half a year, so you must be doing well."

Tears welled in her eyes.

"Aren't you going to get undressed?"

She choked back a sob.

He kicked off his shoes. "Come on, let's make this happen. I don't want him coming in and charging me for additional time because you're in here bawling."

Dwight was never this cold when they were together—except for the final night when he discovered her truth. That night, Junior had humiliated him, and she had broken his heart.

Marlene pulled her shirt over her head.

"Maybe I should put two of these on," Dwight joked as he rolled a condom on. "What do you think?"

The tears came fully now. She didn't bother stopping them as she continued to undress.

Marlene climbed onto the bed, and Dwight mounted her. There was no kissing and no soft words of affection. His eyes flattened as his breathing intensified. He was always a clumsy lover, but he was at least tender. Now, it was as if he was in a race.

She closed her eyes and looked away.

"Open them," Dwight said. "I didn't pay for you to sleep."

Marlene stared up and tried to remember who he was before. But she couldn't. She could only see the sweating, ugly man on top of her now.

Dwight stopped abruptly and slipped out of bed. He grabbed his clothes and went into the bathroom. He hadn't finished, and for that, Marlene was thankful. However, she felt more alone than ever before. She slipped under the bedcovers and pulled them over her head. She curled into a ball and continued to cry.

The door to the bathroom opened, and she heard Dwight pause next to the bed. He stayed there for a moment but didn't say anything. Then he left.

She lost track of time after that. She wasn't sure how many minutes she stayed under the covers. Then she had a terrible realization that if Junior caught her that way, it would not go well. She flipped the covers back and padded into the bathroom. She hurriedly washed her face and returned to the bed with a small towel.

Junior walked in with Amber under his arm. "I bet lover boy caught you by surprise."

She wanted to call him all sorts of names, but what would that accomplish? He'd only make her suffer in some other way. This was her penance. This was what she had to go through because she dared cross him.

"C'mon," Junior said and lifted her chin. "It's not like you hadn't fucked him before. Besides, I made him pay extra, since I knew it was going to be emotionally traumatizing."

"Am I going to see any of that?"

Junior smirked. "You got some lip today." He pulled out a small leather pouch from his jacket. "Maybe I should hold on to your medicine?"

Marlene's eyes locked onto the little leather bag.

"I'm sorry." She scooted to the edge of the bed.

"You say that now, but how do I know you're really sorry?"

"You know I am."

Junior eyed Amber, then jerked his head toward the door. "Go for a stroll, so Marlene can show me how sorry she is."

The younger woman's eyes hardened before leaving.

Junior shook the little pouch in front of her face. "Ready to show me how sorry you really are?"

She reached for him.

***

Marlene awoke several hours later in the hotel room. Junior was gone, and she was alone again. She slowly climbed out of bed, shuffled to the bathroom, and threw up. She then got dressed and left the hotel.

She stopped by Sonnenberg's market and picked up a bag of Doritos and a large bottle of water. Before she was done, she made a detour to the medical aisle.

Back at her apartment, Marlene went directly to the bathroom and ripped open the small box.

She followed the directions and didn't know what to feel when she saw the results.

***

She found Junior at the Hole, a bar along the East Sprague corridor. He was holding court at his table with Amber and a couple of his other girls. Marlene waited her turn until he waved her over. The other girls left, but Amber remained seated next to the big man.

Marlene slid into the booth across from them both. "I'm done."

Junior's brow furrowed. "What are you talking about?"

"I quit."

He laughed, and Amber hesitatingly joined in.

"You can't quit," he said.

"I am."

When she started to slide out of the booth, Junior stabbed his finger at her. "Wait!"

Junior stood but never took his eyes off Marlene. "Amber, get lost."

The other woman scooted out of the booth and went to the other side of the bar. Junior dropped back into his seat.

"Rhonda, baby, I'm sorry."

She shook her head. "Doesn't matter."

"You know I still love you, right?"

Marlene's eyes flicked to Amber. "I could tell."

"Her?" Junior whispered. "I was trying to make you jealous. Get back at you for leaving."

"Let me ask you something."

His eyes softened. "Yeah, sure. Anything."

"Would a man turn out the woman he loves?"

"It's the life we live."

She shook her head. "That's the problem. I don't want to live this life anymore."

Junior rubbed his chin. "You can't walk away. The junk's got you more than I ever will."

"I've got to get out of here, so we'll have a chance against it."

Junior pulled the black pouch from his coat pocket and set it on the table between them.

Marlene's hands shook. "I don't want that."

"You know you do."

"I'm pregnant."

Junior straightened. "You're—"

She nodded.

"How did that happen?"

"How do you think?"

"Who'd you fuck without a condom?"

She raised her eyebrows. He was the only one.

"We'll get you an abortion."

Marlene shook her head, thinking about the first abortion after Junior got her pregnant years ago.

"I'm not doing it."

Junior's lip curled. "You'll do it. And if you don't, I'll beat on your stomach until you piss blood."

"You said you loved me."

He stuck a finger in her face. "You owe me."

"I don't owe you anything."

She slid out of the booth and headed toward the door. Junior followed behind her. "You can't walk out on me!"

"Watch me."

Junior spun her around and slapped her across the mouth.

"Hey," a voice shouted from somewhere in the bar.

"Shut it!" Junior yelled over his shoulder. He dragged her outside. "Leave me again, and I swear I'll kill you."

"Yeah," she said, her voice soft. "I know."

"So, you're staying."

She shook her head. "I'd rather be dead than bring a baby into a life with you."

Junior's nostrils flared, and he raised a hand. Marlene closed her eyes and waited for the blow. When nothing happened, she slowly opened her eyes.

The big man was walking back inside. Several patrons watched her through the window of the bar. A patrol car rounded a corner in the distance.

Marlene hustled down the street to East Sprague Grocery Time. She stood out front, not knowing where to go or who to call for help. Tears ran down her cheeks, and she gnawed on her lip. Her hand went self-consciously to her belly and the daughter she hoped she was carrying. Her body shook as she cried.

The patrol car she'd seen moments before pulled to the curb. A female officer climbed out and approached. Pinned to her uniform was a silver nametag that read *Navarro*.

The officer stood next to Marlene. "You okay, ma'am?"

Marlene shook her head.

"What's wrong?"

"I'm pregnant."

The officer smiled softly. "You shouldn't cry over that."

"I'm scared."

"Of what?"

"Of everything. I have nowhere to go."

"Do you have any family?"

Marlene shook her head.

"Friends?"

Another shake.

"That's okay. No problem. We can find you some help."

Marlene studied the open face of the police officer. Why was she helpful?

The officer gently took Marlene by the elbow and guided her toward the patrol car. "Will this be your first child?"

Marlene nodded.

"You're lucky," Navarro said. "You should be happy. Let's consider this a happy day."

There was movement up the street, and both women looked toward it. Junior stood on the corner near the bar and watched them with interest.

"You know that guy?" the officer asked.

"Yeah."

"He looks like he could be a problem."

"He won't be if I can get out of here."

Officer Navarro's smile was gentle. "Well, let's get you out of here."

She held the door open and assisted Marlene into the backseat. It wasn't the first time Marlene had been in the back of a police car, but it was the first time she'd been there voluntarily. Marlene hoped it would be the last.

The patrol car sped away from the neighborhood.

Marlene didn't bother looking back. Her life was now going to be elsewhere.

Forgive Us Our Sins

"He's in the wind," Dave Elmendorf whispered as he made a vodka tonic. "Up to a month ago, he stopped in at his usual haunts, and then it's like he just vanished."

I snapped my fingers. "Poof. Gone."

"That's the word." Dave slid the glass tumbler across the countertop. "Rumor is he skipped town."

I sipped my replenished drink before asking in a low voice, "Where would he run?"

Dave shrugged. "He never goes anywhere and has never been anywhere."

"Was he in trouble? Maybe owed someone money?"

"Trouble?" Dave whispered. "He had a lot of it, but nobody said anything about him owing money."

Dave's network of bartenders was surprisingly effective for intel on hard-to-find lowlifes.

"Who you guys talking about?" Chandra, the woman seated next to me, leaned in with evident excitement.

"Shhhh." Dave held a finger to his lips. He was a thick man with short red hair and thick glasses. His T-shirt strained against his biceps and barrel chest. Most people would be wise to listen when they're told to be quiet.

We were in The Tiptoe Lounge, the bar in Dave's basement. It was an after-hours joint for friends and his best customers, whom he wanted to call friends.

Dave was the lead bartender at Mulligan's, a North Monroe dive where all sorts of characters frequent. It attracts a motley collection of derelicts, divorcees, and trust-fund babies slumming for trouble. Dave had worked there for almost twenty years and lives within walking distance.

I liked Mulligan's because of its cheap drinks, dark corners, and proximity to my former employer, the Spokane County Sheriff's Office. Dave and I had been friendly for years, as much as a bartender and a customer could be. When he learned that I unceremoniously left the department, he invited me back to the lounge. That's when we became friends.

Chandra's smile grew with a mixture of anticipation and whiskey. "Aw, come on, who are you talking about?" Her voice had quieted with the hint of conspiracy.

"Your ex," I whispered.

She laughed loudly—a bark really—and slapped her hands together. "I wish!"

"*Shhh!*" The entire lounge had shushed her now.

The illuminated *Quiet!* sign was on, which meant Maggie wasn't working the hospital's late shift. She hated the Tiptoe and most of Dave's friends. The tales of debauchery in the basement were legendary, some that I'd witnessed and some that I wished I'd seen. Maggie didn't appreciate that kind of behavior in her house.

No music played tonight, and everyone talked in hushed tones. Waking Maggie meant a quick end to the evening's fun, and none of us wanted that. Even though she was a foot shorter and a hundred pounds lighter than Dave, she kept him on a short leash.

Chandra pushed her empty tumbler toward Dave but kept her watery eyes locked on me. In the low light of Dave's basement, she was starting to look vaguely pretty. "You really looking for Lorne?"

"That's right."

"Is he in trouble?"

"Could be."

She smiled and patted my knee, leaving her hand there when she was done. "That's good."

"You don't like him?" Dave asked.

She studied me. "I'm trading up."

Her full name was Chandra Ramona Culbertson, and I initially located her at the Northern Rail Pub in Hillyard. I bought her a drink to get her talking. However, I didn't like how the locals eyed us, so I suggested moving to Mulligan's. She accepted quicker than I expected. A couple more drinks there, and Dave invited me back to The Tiptoe Lounge. Chandra was eager to tag along.

I hadn't asked her age, but I guessed she was pushing fifty. All those years, coupled with a heavy smoking habit, had not been kind to her skin. She was a smallish woman with hair the color of buttered toast if the bread had flecks of silver in it. Throughout the night, I had an ongoing argument with myself about whether she was attractive or not. So far, I kept falling on the negative side of that equation.

Initially, Chandra didn't talk about herself, although she loosened as we drank. Whenever I asked about her boyfriend, though, she waved me off and said something under her breath. She finally admitted she broke up with him six weeks before—two weeks before he went missing.

Dave refilled her glass with Wild Turkey and ice. She sipped it, pulled her lips back in a grimace, then replaced it with a smile that wasn't much better. "You gonna make sure I get home?"

"Sure, but I still have business to discuss with Dave."

"But you're buying my drinks, right?"

"You bet."

Her eyes drooped a bit, and her tongue darted across her lips. She rubbed my leg now. "You're sweet."

"That's what I've heard." I chuckled and leaned toward her. She was indeed attractive.

From the corner of my eye, I could see Dave shaking his head.

***

In the morning, Chandra looked like hell.

The long night with Wild Turkey didn't help, and the light of day certainly made things worse, but the reality was Chandra Culbertson was a rough woman. Dave had seen me do worse, although I'd never brought them back to his after-hours joint.

As quietly as I could, I slid out of bed to put my pants on.

I cringed when she asked, "Where you going so early?"

"Need to get moving. Long day ahead."

She pushed herself upright against the headboard, exposing herself. I turned away and put my shirt on.

"Are you really looking for Lorne?"

"Yeah."

"He took off, you know?"

"You believe that?"

"Everybody says so."

Still not looking at her, I sat on the edge of the bed to put my shoes on. "What makes you think he's gone?"

"He would have called by now. Even if I didn't want him to, he would have. He's a tomcat."

Without looking back, I asked, "When's the last time he contacted you?"

I heard her light a cigarette and exhale before I could smell the smoke. "More than a month."

"Have you tried to contact him?"

"No," she said with a snort. "I don't want that man back in my life."

"Was he in trouble with anyone?"

Chandra exhaled, and smoke appeared over my shoulder. "Not that I know of, but he never told me his business. What I do know is that he's a bad man, but for the life of me, I can't stop myself from getting with him when he comes around. If he's gone, then it's good for me."

I stood with a slight grunt.

"If you find him, do me a favor?"

"What's that?" I faced her and pulled my car keys from my pocket.

Her smile was laced with a former lover's cruelty. "Tell him we made it."

***

My car was outside Chandra's apartment, parked partially on the sidewalk. It was clear now that I shouldn't have driven us home.

"I'm an idiot," I muttered to myself.

"You won't get an argument from me."

I turned to find Detective Vaughn Hill behind me. In his late forties, Hill stood a few inches taller than me, but I carried twenty more pounds than him. Hill wore blue jeans and a polo shirt. His gun and badge were on his belt.

"What are you doing here?" I asked.

"None of your business. What are you doing here?"

"None of your business."

Hill spat on the ground, then headed toward Chandra's apartment building.

At the time I was forced out of the sheriff's department, I was the sergeant of the Major Crimes unit, which handled homicides and robberies. The detectives of this unit were the best, and they came with egos matching their talent. Unfortunately, I had been an average patrolman and had about the same skill level as a detective before making sergeant. If I'm anything, I'm realistic about my abilities.

Vaughn Hill, the most vocal detective, wrote a series of complaints to the upper administration and urged his cronies to do the same. I was his supervisor, but he had it out for me and let me know it. In the end, Vaughn and the other detectives got their way, and I accepted the administration's "suggestion" of early retirement.

I quickly got in my car and left. The last thing I wanted was for Hill to catch me watching him. I wouldn't give him the satisfaction.

***

"You get anything on Lorne Ford?"

Ethan Raynes leaned back in his faux leather chair and crossed his hands behind his head. He was in his late fifties, soft around the middle, and now a paper tiger. However, in his earlier days, Ethan was a man to be feared when he worked the street.

"I found his ex, Chandra Culbertson."

"She give you anything?"

"Not really."

The way Ethan studied me, I had a fleeting thought that he knew about Chandra and me. It wasn't my finest investigative work, and I would be embarrassed if he knew what I had done. "That's too bad. I was hoping she would have given him up, and this case would be a slam dunk."

"I don't think it's a viable lead."

"You don't think—what's that mean?"

"She doesn't know where he's at."

"Why didn't you just say that? Where to next?"

"I've got some history with his mother. So I figured I'd try her next."

"Good deal. Wrap this up."

"You still haven't told me why we're looking for this guy. Who's our client? Why do they want him found?"

"Let it go, George. Our client wants to remain anonymous. Their reasons for finding this turd are their own. We get paid to find him—not to ask why."

Ethan's tone had a finality in it, and I didn't see any need to push it.

***

Nancy Ford had been a career criminal, and in her heyday, she was notorious.

She had her fingers in all sorts of criminal enterprises. Stolen checks, food stamp fraud, off-track betting, promoting prostitution, and fencing of stolen property, to name a handful. If there was a profit to be found, she was in it.

Nancy was a smart woman, avoiding both physical crime and violent men. Unfortunately, no matter how intelligent a criminal is, sooner or later, the law catches up with them.

She did some time in the Airway Heights Correctional Center. While there, she found Jesus somewhere around her fifty-fourth birthday. When she turned her life around, she got work as a grocery clerk, went to church on Sundays, and married a God-fearing man who did his best to take care of her.

Nancy tried her best to atone for her sins—all but one of them.

She opened the door after I knocked. Her steel gray hair was pulled back in a bun. She had put on some weight since the last time I'd seen her. "Sergeant Moore," she said.

"It's just George now. I'm retired."

Nancy's brow furrowed. "Ain't you a little young to be retired?"

"Wasn't exactly my choice."

"Sorry to hear that," she said with more sympathy than I would have expected. Maybe the church was having a positive effect. "What's a forcibly retired police sergeant doin' at my doorstep?"

"Looking for your son."

She sighed, then rubbed a hand over her face. "What's he done this time?"

"Nothing that I know of. I've been hired to find him."

"You some sort of private investigator or something?"

"Or something."

"Who's looking for him?"

"Now, Nancy, you know I can't tell you that."

She glanced up and down the street, making sure her neighbors weren't watching this exchange. "He's not a good man, George. I'm not a fool. However, if I did know where my son was—and I'm not saying I do—but *if* I did, I wouldn't tell you."

"I understand."

She searched my eyes for a moment, not saying anything.

"Have you talked with him recently?"

Nancy remained silent.

"You see, I'm asking because no one has seen him around. The word on the street is that Lorne was here one day and gone the next. Does that sound like him?"

"He can do what he likes. He's a full-grown man."

"I hear you, but I'm asking you to consider my questions." I held my hand over my heart like I was pledging allegiance to the flag. It seemed a motion of sincerity she would understand. "Is it like Lorne—your boy—to suddenly disappear? Is it like him to stop talking to his family and friends? He doesn't have a job, so no one there is going to report him missing."

She lowered her eyes, seemingly lost in thought. When she looked at me again, her gaze had softened. "I'm pretty sure he would have called if he was going somewhere. I ain't spoken to him in several weeks. Now that you're here, I'll admit I'm worried."

We made some small talk after that. Nothing of significance. Just remembering some of the good times when she made me chase her all over town. It was worth a couple of laughs.

As I turned to leave, an unmarked patrol car drove by. I couldn't see who was behind the wheel.

"Did you call for backup?" Nancy asked. "Worried about fighting with me again?"

She chuckled as the unmarked unit turned the corner and disappeared.

***

It was a little after five when I returned to the offices of County Investigations. Ethan was gone, as was the receptionist. I was there to file a report on my conversation with Nancy Ford. Just like police work, private investigation was based upon the detailing of one's activities.

As I stood in the middle of the office, I thought about my conversation with Ethan concerning our client. The anonymous bit bothered me. I'd done work for Ethan before and frequently didn't know the actual name of the client. However, they would generally be referred to as "the husband" or "the guy's boss."

Something didn't smell right with the disappearance of Lorne Ford and our client's anonymity.

I walked into Ethan's office and opened the file cabinet behind his desk. It only took a couple of minutes of searching to find the Ford file.

On the right side of the file was my report from The Tiptoe Lounge. A second report would soon be there from the conversation with Nancy. On the left-hand side of the folder was the datasheet. It showed the name and address of the person who requested the "find" on Lorne.

I copied her info into my notebook and went back to my office to write my report.

***

When I finished the statement, it was after six. I locked up and headed to the parking lot. Next to my car was an unmarked patrol car. It was the same one that had driven past Nancy Ford's house. I slowly approached the police vehicle, not wanting to spook whoever was inside. But as I got closer, I could see no one behind the wheel.

Some movement reflected in the driver's window, but I didn't react fast enough. I was shoved against the patrol car and pinned. My right arm was wrenched behind my back.

I grunted and struggled to get free. A punch to my left kidney took the fight from me, and I dropped to a knee.

"Want to throw hands, George?"

I looked over my shoulder and saw Detective Vaughn Hill. He leaned into me, pressing me into the car.

"Get off."

As he stepped back, Hill pushed me once more against the car.

I stood and turned around. Briefly, I thought about fighting him, but Hill was in better shape and would easily win. As I said, I'm realistic about my abilities. "Why are you following me?"

"Whatever you're looking for—let it go."

"What am I looking for?"

Hill's punch was fast, and it sunk deep into my gut. I fell to my hands and knees, sucking for air. He opened his car door, hitting me in the butt and knocking me entirely to the ground.

He backed his car out of the parking stall and drove away.

***

Our cars sat alongside each other, the driver's sides near each other. The windows were down, allowing us to have a conversation without leaving our cars.

Corporal Craig Dobson bent over the keyboard of his in-car computer. "Confirm the spelling of the last name."

"Bennett," I said and spelled it out for him. "Angela Elizabeth." I gave him her birthday, which was a couple of months ago, making her thirty-four years old. She was listed as the client in the Lorne Ford file.

"Got it. She lives in the valley."

"Any history?"

"Some traffic stuff. All minor. And a rape victim report."

"When was that?"

"Fifteen years ago."

"Who was the suspect?"

Craig typed some more before announcing, "Lorne L. Ford."

"Ford?"

"That guy's a piece of squeeze."

"Was he convicted?"

Craig turned back to his computer. "No."

"I don't remember that case."

"You probably wouldn't. It occurred in the city, so their team handled it."

I thought about asking Craig if he heard anything lately concerning Vaughn Hill, but friendships frequently change inside law enforcement departments. Even though Craig and I had been friends for years, that didn't mean that he hadn't become close with Hill since I left.

"Thanks for the info," I said.

"You owe me lunch," Craig said. "Some beers, too."

"Name the time," I said and drove away.

***

Angela Bennett lived in Spokane Valley just off Sullivan Road in a newer apartment complex. After I introduced myself, she asked, "Why are you here?"

"I'm working your case, and I'm having trouble locating a guy who I think should be easy to find."

Angela crossed her arms. "So, what? You come to my house tonight to complain? To ask for more money?"

"I came to ask why you want to find Lorne Ford."

"That's no business of yours. You work *for* me. I don't have to explain myself."

I rubbed my chin, studying her. She was an attractive woman with a thin frame and elf-like features. Her chocolate-copper hair was cut short in a wedge style.

"I know what he did to you."

Her eyes widened for a moment, but she set her jaw, leaving her lips to tremble. Red blotches appeared on her cheeks. "You know nothing."

"I'm trying to find him and earn my pay, but I have some questions."

"So?"

"He's vanished."

Her eyes slanted, and the trembling in her lips stopped. "What do you think that means?" The way she asked it showed more concern for Lorne Ford than I thought possible.

"I don't know, but it's troubling."

She turned and walked into her apartment. She sat on the couch and held her head in her hands. As I waited for her to get control of herself, I scanned the photographs on the wall. All of them were of Angela and a man in his late forties.

"Your boyfriend?" I nodded toward the pictures.

"Fiancé."

"Does he live here?"

"Sometimes."

We watched each other for a while, neither piercing the quiet with a question. She was afraid of me being there, not physically, but something else.

"You're afraid your boyfriend knows. About the rape." When she didn't say anything, I pressed forward. "No, wait, that's not true. He already knows. You told him about it, but he didn't take it well."

She reset her jaw, and the look of defiance returned, but tears now welled in her eyes.

I moved to the chair across from her and sat. "Did he say he would hurt Lorne?"

Angela rolled her lips into her mouth and shut her eyes.

"You couldn't go to the police, could you? So that's why you came to us to find Lorne?"

She slowly nodded as several tears dropped from behind closed eyelids.

"You want to do what? Warn him?"

Angela opened her eyes then. "What he did to me was wrong. It was evil. He's evil. It's taken a lot of years to get over. I'll never forget it, but I have forgiven him. It hasn't been easy to get there, but it's the Christian thing to do. Can you understand that?"

"Why do you want to protect him?"

She shook her head. "You've got it wrong, Mr. Moore. I don't want to protect him. I couldn't care less about what happens to that man. However, I can't be with a man who will intentionally harm another person. Not after what I've been through."

***

The next morning, I waited in the parking lot until Ethan Raynes arrived in his Mercedes. After he parked and climbed out, I approached him.

"You're here early." Ethan opened the rear door of his car.

"Vaughn Hill is Angela Bennett's fiancé." My words were rushed as if they'd been dammed up waiting for his arrival. Perhaps they had been.

Ethan grabbed his briefcase from the backseat and closed the door. "Say that again."

"Vaughn Hill," I said slowly, "is our client's fiancé."

"When did you find this out?"

"Last night."

"How—"

"She told me. I figure this means Vaughn killed Lorne Ford."

He eyed me with something close to contempt.

"That's why she hired us," I said. "Think about it."

Ethan walked toward the building, and I dropped in behind him. "Listen. Here's how I got it figured—"

"Stop talking, George."

"But I figure that Vaughn—"

He spun around and stuck a finger in my face. "Not another word—not one—until we are inside my office. Do you understand?"

I nodded and followed him inside. Ethan slapped his briefcase against the side of his desk and dropped into his chair. "Okay, George. I've only got a question for you, and it's a doozy. Can you guess what it is?"

"I read her file—the one in your office."

Ethan shook his head. "She wanted to remain anonymous. She said her fiancé was connected to law enforcement but asked if we could leave it at that. I told her we would. You made me into a liar, George."

"I was getting nowhere. So I thought talking to her would get me a break. And it did."

He rubbed his forehead for a moment, then sighed. "Lay it out, but it better be good. You're on thin ice."

I filled him in on what I learned about Lorne Ford from my friend on the department. "When I went to Angela's apartment, I saw photos of her and Vaughn together. That's when she confirmed Vaughn was her fiancé. She also admitted she told him about what happened with Ford."

Ethan frowned.

"Vaughn got upset and went looking for Ford."

"Wait. You know this how?"

"That's what she said. That's why she's worried. That's why she hired us. She wants to warn Ford."

"That's not enough to prove the Vaughn killed a man."

"He's been following me."

"Who? Vaughn?"

"I saw him outside Lorne's ex-girlfriend's house, and I'm pretty sure he drove by while I was at his mom's place. And last night in our parking lot, he jumped me. Right there." I pointed outside. "He told me to stop looking into whatever I was after."

Ethan leaned back in his chair and crossed his arms. "Yesterday afternoon, he stopped in to shoot the breeze. I didn't think anything of it. Vaughn and I always got along well."

"He's covering his tracks."

"You're stretching. Vaughn Hill is a good man."

"He's an asshole."

"He'd say the same about you."

I tsked. "He's behind Lorne's disappearance. I know it."

Ethan exhaled slowly and put his hands on the edge of his desk. "Slow down and step back. You're letting your history with the man blind you. This is what happened on the department, and it cost you your job."

"*He* cost me my job."

"Which is why you're blinded to the possibility of him being innocent."

"I'll get him to confess."

"Maybe he hasn't done anything."

"I'm not wrong."

"You're not even considering other possibilities."

"I'm right, Ethan. Wait and see."

I hurried out of his office, pretending I didn't hear him calling my name.

***

Vaughn Hill ate lunch at Rosie's Diner on Washington Street. It's where he dined on Thursdays while I was on the department, and he hadn't changed his routine since I left.

I slid into the booth across from him. Hill lifted his eyes, then carefully put down his sandwich. "The hell do you think you're doing?"

"We should talk." I shooed away the waitress when she came by.

Hill's eyes filled with suspicion. "Make it quick."

"I work with Ethan Raynes now."

"No kidding. I found you in the parking lot." Hill leaned over the table and took a bite of his sandwich. "Or have you forgotten?" he mumbled through a mouthful of food.

"I'm working a case, and I thought maybe you could help."

Hill put his sandwich down again. "Still bumbling your way through life on the goodwill of others."

"You need a new routine."

"It was true then." He brushed his hands together and wiped crumbs onto the table. "Still true now."

"You didn't have to write the chief about it."

His smile lacked mirth. "If you want an apology, you're not getting one. You were sloppy and lazy."

"At times."

"You could have been better if you applied yourself."

"Not everyone can be you, Vaughn."

"With your work ethic, it's no surprise those wives of yours didn't keep you around."

I shook my head. "Brutally honest, as always."

"No need to sugarcoat it. We're not friends."

"The help I came for is very specific. Only you can give it to me."

"It's time you go."

"I know you wouldn't go out of your way for me—"

He sipped his water and waited for the punch line.

"But I figured you might give a little help for sweet, little Angela."

Hill dried his lips with a napkin. "What are you talking about?"

"Angela hired us to find Lorne Ford. You know who he is?"

"I know who Ford is," he said, his voice low. "Every cop knows him. Why would Angela do something like that?"

"She wanted to warn him that he might be in danger."

He leaned in slightly and focused tighter on me. "What are you talking about?" His words were slow and precise.

"I was surprised to see you in the pictures in her living room."

"You were in her apartment?" The corner of his lip twitched.

"You've gotta be, what, fifteen years older than her? You probably add some stability to her life. You looked happy in those photos. Maybe she has abandonment issues."

The edge of his mouth twitched again.

"She said when you found out what happened to her that it deeply affected you."

Hill remained silent, but his right hand balled into a fist.

"Ford should have gone to jail," I said, "but for whatever reason, they couldn't convict."

"Lousy police work is what it was. I saw the report."

"I'm sure it was. Everyone's work is lousy compared to yours—isn't it, Vaughn? What you've failed to realize is that Angela has moved on from that moment, and she doesn't want you to hurt him. She shared what happened so you would understand who she was."

His jaw muscles flexed once. Then he forced the edges of his mouth down to stop them from twitching.

"It doesn't matter now, does it?"

Hill's gaze drifted about the restaurant. "I don't know what you're talking about."

"I'm not wearing a wire, Vaughn. I'm not here to jam you up. I don't care if Ford is ever found. Knowing how organized you are in your work, I'm sure you covered every base."

"What's wrong with you?"

"Your fiancé is scared something bad happened to Ford and thinks you might be responsible for it."

Hill's face reddened. "I haven't done anything."

"Tell me you did it, and I'll drop my investigation."

"I'm not saying shit to you," Hill said through clenched teeth.

"That's odd. I figured you would have said you didn't kill him or something else along those lines."

"How about we step outside, and I kick your ass?"

"Let's not. I submitted my report to Angela before coming here. It states that Lorne Ford has vanished in such a way that she'll put the pieces together. I reported my interviews with his mother and his ex-girlfriend and what his friends think about his disappearance. I even put in there that I had several run-ins with you and that you assaulted and threatened me."

His face slackened. "You've made a mistake, George. I didn't do anything."

"Why'd you tell me to stay away from searching for Lorne? Why'd you hit me?"

"Fine." Hill's lips pinched before he continued. "I was looking for him, but you kept showing up wherever I went. I didn't know what you were doing."

"So, you hit me and threatened me?"

Hill rubbed his face with a hand. "It's no secret that I don't like you."

"No secret," I agreed.

"Seeing you got me a little wound up."

"You hit me."

The detective shrugged. "Things happen."

I exhaled dismissively. "No, they don't. Which is why Angela's going to wonder if you put Ford in the ground."

He leaned in and forcefully said, "I didn't do that."

"It looks like you're running around, making sure all your loose ends are tied off."

"That's not what I'm doing. You came here."

"Angela will never know for sure, and that's going to eat at her. Tear her up inside."

The glare in Hill's eyes faded for a moment. "Don't do this, George. She's a nice girl, and we've got a good thing going."

"Poor Angela." I made a sad face. "Living with the fear that her boyfriend is a monster, just like the criminal who raped her."

"You bastard." Spittle remained on his lower lip.

"I may not have been as good a detective as you, Vaughn," I said as I slid out of the booth. "But I don't have the blood of the innocent man on my hands."

"He wasn't innocent!" Hill slapped the table. His plate and silverware clattered noisily.

The other diners in the restaurant turned to watch. Hill became aware of the eyes upon us and turned back to me. He lowered his voice. "I never found him, George. Had I, I probably would have put him in the ground. But I didn't. He's still out there somewhere doing God knows what to God knows who."

I leaned in and whispered, "You found him, and you killed him. And that's what my report suggests."

Hill grabbed the edge of the table as if he were trying to stabilize his world.

I straightened. "Now, I could go to Angela and say something like I found Ford and that everything is okay. Maybe give her some peace. Allow you both some happiness."

A flash of hope moved through Hill's eyes, like a drowning man desperately reaching for a life preserver.

"But as you said, we're not friends. So, I won't do that for you."

Something died behind the detective's eyes, which caused me to smile.

"I'm not sure you remember this," I said, "but what was the only thing you ever complimented me on in all of those complaints to the administration?"

Hill pushed his plate away.

"My report writing. You always said I wrote nice, clean reports. Guess you're going to find out how true that statement is now."

He jumped from his booth, grabbed me by the shirt, and punched me several times in the face.

Before the police arrived, the diner's patrons had pulled Hill from me, and he had left the restaurant.

***

A couple of months later, I made it back to The Tiptoe Lounge. The music was on that night. Maggie was pulling a double shift at the hospital, which meant the party would go late into the morning.

Dave slid another vodka tonic across the counter as I watched two women study three guys murmuring and sipping dark drinks.

"So, what happened after he hit you?" Dave asked as he wiped down the bar.

I tasted my drink. It was heavy on the vodka, light on the tonic. In other words, perfect. "Hill was charged with misdemeanor assault."

"You pressed charges?"

"Damn right, I did, but I kept my mouth shut when the officers asked what set Ford off."

"Why do that?"

"I wanted to see if he would tell them what I accused him of."

"And did he?"

"Nope." I sipped my vodka again. "After he calmed down, Hill came back to the diner and admitted he struck me. But he clammed up on why. The department's brass knew about the bad blood between us, and they figured I said something to provoke him."

Dave stopped wiping the bar and straightened. "His keeping quiet made him look guilty of killing Ford. I mean, don't you think?"

"It looked that way—yeah."

"Huh." He leaned over and started wiping again. In a moment, he stopped and eyed me. "Looked that way?"

I rubbed my finger along the side of my glass. "A few weeks after the fight with Hill, Lorne's mother contacted me. He called on her birthday."

Dave's mouth dropped open.

"Seems he had met some girl and ran off to New Orleans. Nancy—his mom—said he sounded drugged out, but that it was still nice to hear from him. We had a nice conversation. She reminded me of a couple other funny moments we had."

"Did you let anyone know?"

My brow furrowed. "About our funny moments?"

"No," Dave said, "about Ford being alive. Did you let your boss know? Or the girl, at least?"

"I thought about telling my boss, but that would mean more paperwork. Besides, I already got paid for that job, and he would have called Hill. In the end, how would that help me? Hill's jammed up for the assault in the diner and might lose his job. If that happens, it's a nice turn of events. At worst, it's tarnished his do-gooder reputation. I don't want to give him any possible excuse to weasel out."

Dave's brow furrowed. "But it's the truth."

I shrugged.

"What about Angela?"

I slowly turned my glass on the bar. "I occasionally check on her. You know, to see how she's doing. She's still sad after breaking it off with Vaughn. She didn't want to be with a guy who's a monster. She can't trust the man, especially since he won't admit what he did to Ford."

Dave's mouth slowly opened. "Wow."

"She's getting better, though. I bring her chocolates and little things to cheer her up, which she seems to appreciate."

"That's cold."

"What do you mean? I'm not trying to sleep with her or anything."

"You're not?"

"She's not over her last boyfriend yet."

"Like that's ever stopped you." Something resembling displeasure masked his face.

"True." I clinked my drink against his empty glass. "But it's better to be a friend and let it happen naturally, then try to force it and be disappointed. That way, I don't get my feelings hurt. I always work better in the friend zone, anyway."

"Wow," Dave muttered again. He snatched his bar towel and walked off.

I sipped my drink and watched him go. It was good to be realistic about one's abilities.

Cry Uncle

Carl Spencer stood barefoot in his living room. He repeatedly scrunched his toes and relaxed them, feeling the carpet beneath him. He smiled and sipped his Cabernet Sauvignon. For Carl, life was good.

He lived alone on Spokane's South Hill in a home that had been in his family for three generations. A child of wealth, Spencer's life was carefree due to the trust fund left him by his parents. Careful investments by the fund managers had allowed Spencer, now thirty-eight years of age, to avoid the very pedestrian demands of work.

The pursuits of art, music, and wine filled most of his days. He had no steady woman, as the burden of the female species detracted from his real interests.

Spencer now danced in his home while the music of Vivaldi echoed through the rooms.

His spirits were light—a date earlier in the night went well. He had taken a younger woman to dinner. He had no interest in her, but appearances had to be maintained. After dinner, he extricated himself from her advances and made it home early enough to enjoy a glass of wine before the evening's real entertainment.

Spencer thought he could still smell the young woman's perfume on him as he moved around the living room. He wrinkled his nose at the thought.

The music swelled, and his smile returned. His eyes remained closed as he danced slowly, rhythmically—

Abruptly, the music stopped.

Spencer opened his eyes, set his wineglass down on a nearby table, and headed toward the stereo system at the end of the hallway.

The power to the stereo was off. He pressed the button, and the components lit up. He pushed the play button, and the music started again. Spencer shrugged at the inconvenience and turned around.

Standing in the hallway, blocking any escape, was a big man dressed in dark blue polyester pants, a bulky black jacket, and a black ski mask. Black leather gloves covered the man's fists.

Spencer stepped back and raised his hands in defense. "Whatever you want, take it."

The big man said three words. "Where's the girl?"

"Whatever you—"

Spencer never finished the sentence as the big man moved quickly and overwhelmed him.

***

When Spencer woke, his jaw hurt, and he couldn't move. Duct tape secured his arms and legs to one of the handcrafted dining room chairs.

The man in the ski mask crossed the room and slowly, painfully, pulled the construction tape from Spencer's mouth.

Once it was removed, he exclaimed, "Why are—" but the man punched him in the chest.

Not accustomed to pain, Spencer passed out once more.

***

"Where's the girl?"

Spencer moved his head and opened his eyes. When the realization of his predicament returned to him, his lips trembled. "Girl?"

"Tracy Mossman."

"Who?"

The man slapped Spencer hard across the face. He squealed and thrashed about in the chair.

"Where's the girl?"

"I don't know what you're talking about." Carl closed his eyes, waiting for the next blow. He didn't have to wait long.

The big man drove a fist into his ribs, cracking one. Spencer screamed.

"Where's the girl?"

Spencer cried and shook his head. Spittle covered his lips, and mucus ran from his nose.

The big man pulled his fist back for another strike.

Spencer turned his face away and screamed, "No!"

The man froze with his arm cocked.

With tears running down his cheeks, Spencer whispered, "The basement."

The big man slowly lowered his hand.

"The basement," Spencer muttered and nodded.

The man yanked a strip of duct tape from the roll and covered Spencer's mouth.

***

A cursory walk through the finished basement didn't reveal the girl. Under the mask, the big man's lip curled as he believed Carl Spencer had lied. He struggled to control his anger and searched again.

Each room was furnished in a different style. It was in the last bedroom that the big man stopped. He stepped to the doorway to compare the depths of the walls. The bedroom's southern wall was several feet closer to him than the end of the hallway.

A dresser stood in front of the wall. The big man pushed the piece of furniture to the side and revealed a small door with two handles. He jerked on the handles, and the door popped free from the wall.

Inside was a small hideaway with no lighting. A four-year-old girl lay inside with her hands and feet tied. Her blonde hair was dirty and matted. Her eyes widened with fear as she stared at the masked man.

He squatted and reached out for her but stopped.

Tears streamed down the girl's face. She had been missing for three days, so he hadn't expected to find her alive.

His mouth went dry, and his heart pounded. He thought of removing his mask to ease her fears. He wanted to pick her up, hold her close, and let her know that no one would ever hurt her again. The big man did none of those things.

They stared at each other for a moment before the little girl whispered, "Please."

"You're safe."

He stood and left the room.

***

Carl Spencer didn't hear the big man until it was too late.

If he had heard him, Spencer could have clenched his jaw and twisted away from the blow. Instead, he looked up, his eyes red from crying.

Duct tape muffled his screams.

The big man's first punch broke Spencer's jaw. The second blow broke his nose. The third rendered Spencer unconscious.

***

The big man made his way through the home. In the bedrooms on the main floor, he pulled drawers out of dressers and dumped their contents onto the floor. In the home office, he rummaged through the desk, throwing its contents around. He found a small stash of collectible coins that he took.

He stopped and looked around the house. The mess almost seemed appropriate, with one exception.

The big man locked the front door with the deadbolt, exited the house through the rear, and circled back around to the entrance. He broke the light over the stairs.

It took two kicks before the front door burst open and splintered the doorjamb. He had initially entered the house through an unlocked basement window, passing the room where the little girl was hidden.

The man walked into the kitchen, picked up Spencer's cell phone, and dialed 911. As a dispatcher asked what his emergency was, he set the phone on the counter.

At the front door, he dropped the collectible coins and left the house.

His car was a couple of blocks away. As he walked toward it, he removed the mask, the bulky black jacket, and his gloves. The moonless night was so dark that he wasn't worried about anyone seeing him—not anymore.

The man stored the clothing in the trunk. When he climbed in, he started the car, which immediately activated its radio.

"—a nine-one-one call from a cell phone registered to 2301 South Manito Boulevard. The line is still open. No noise can be heard in the background."

Two patrol units radioed that they were heading to the call.

The big man picked up the microphone from the dashboard and keyed it. "Charlie Three Twelve, I'm a few blocks away from that call. Show me on scene."

"Copy," the police dispatcher responded.

The big man drove the two blocks to the address, climbed out of his patrol car, and trotted toward the house. He ignored the usual precaution of a slow and cautious approach. He activated the radio on his hip, then called dispatch.

"Charlie Three Twelve."

"Three Twelve, go ahead."

"There's an open door with signs of forced entry."

"Copy."

"Have the other units step it up but come in silent."

The other units announced via radio that they were coming into the area. The big man waited by the front door with his gun drawn.

Patience was his friend now. There was no need to hurry. He stared in through the open doorway, knowing where Spencer sat duct-taped and unconscious. He knew where the little girl lay, bound and crying.

Footsteps soon approached the house. He glanced back to see Officer Sharon Hall and Corporal Kyle Banks.

Banks put his hand on the big man's shoulder. "How are you holding up, Len?"

"I'm fine."

"We'll find her," Sharon said.

Pointing at the splintered doorjamb, Len said, "There's forced entry, and it looks like they dropped something on the way out." He motioned to the coins scattered about the entryway. "There's no noise from inside, but I didn't want to enter by myself."

Sharon whispered, "We should call for a dog to search the house."

Len imagined a police dog finding the little girl in the basement. He wouldn't take the chance the dog would bite. "No. Let's go in."

Banks nodded in agreement and keyed his microphone. After giving his call sign, he said, "Restrict this channel. We're entering the house."

"Spokane Police Department," Sharon yelled into the house. "Come out with your hands up." When no one did, she hollered the same thing once more.

"Ready?" Banks asked.

All three of them entered with their guns drawn. Sharon went first with Len second. Banks brought up the rear. Almost as soon as they cleared the front entry, Sharon found Carl Spencer. He was still passed out in his chair.

"Holy crap," muttered Sharon. She keyed her shoulder microphone. "Start an ambulance. We've got one with signs of assault."

Banks covered the stairwell to the basement as Sharon and Len cleared the rest of the main floor. When they finished, Len said, "Kyle and I will get the basement."

Sharon nodded and moved to assist Carl Spencer.

Len motioned at Banks to lead the way, and the corporal moved on. It was important for someone else to make the discovery. Banks was first in the back room and found the shoved aside dresser.

"What the hell is that?"

He hurried forward to find the little girl inside the cubbyhole. He glanced back and asked, "Is this her?"

Len holstered his gun as he knelt. He removed the binds around the little girl's hands and feet before picking her up. She wrapped her arms around his neck and clung to him tightly.

"You're safe," he said once more and carried her out of the house.

***

The news broke mid-morning and interrupted the talk shows and soap operas.

Initially reported as a home invasion robbery, the call turned into the discovery of the kidnapped and bound missing girl, Tracy Mossman. She had been a nightly story on the local news broadcasts.

The reports also mentioned that several officers, including her uncle, Leonard Mossman, had found the girl. She was later reunited with her mother at a local hospital.

The homeowner, Carl Spencer, was arrested for kidnapping but was currently under medical care. He had suffered a broken jaw, nose, and ribs at the hands of the intruder. He would be transferred to the Spokane County Jail upon his release from the hospital.

Spokane Police Chief Liam Dillon held a press conference to praise the officers involved in the search and recovery of Tracy Mossman. "Carl Spencer was a person of interest in her disappearance, but we didn't have enough for a warrant. Had the break-in not occurred, we would not have recovered that little girl."

The news report stations ended their coverage of the chief's press conference with his statement, "We got lucky today."

The Return of Jack O'Day

Jack O'Day yanked open the heavy wooden door to the Howard Street Smuggler's Club. A whiff of cigarette smoke and a blast of tinny music greeted his entrance. Even though he'd never been there before, Jack strolled in like he owned the place. It was the strut of a victor, something he hadn't experienced much in his twenty-five years.

It was shortly after five, and most of the bar stools were filled. He squeezed in between a hard-hatted construction worker and a yuppie showing off an expensive suit.

The bartender, a late-fifties Italian with bushy eyebrows, tossed a coaster onto the hardwood and lazily asked, "What'll you have?"

"Whiskey with a beer back."

On the television set hanging above the bar, Dan Rather appeared to drone on about a war somewhere. The sound was off to not compete with the jukebox as it played Huey Lewis and the News's "Hip to Be Square."

Jack eyed the patrons lining the bar. They all seemed like citizens grabbing some liquid courage before going home to toe the line with their better halves. That was fine with him. He wasn't looking for trouble. He only wanted a couple of drinks and to kill some time. Then he'd slip out of this town like a thief in the night.

Well, something like that.

The bartender set his drink in front of him, then snapped open a can of Olympia. After the Italian announced a total, Jack removed a cash roll from his pocket and peeled a ten from it. The bartender scooped it up deftly and left to make change.

The yuppie studied the wad of money until he noticed Jack glaring back. A nervous chuckle was followed by a muttered, "Sorry."

"I remind you of someone?"

"I said I was sorry."

"Keep it that way."

Citizens, Jack thought. Always good for one thing—backing down in a pinch.

He kicked back the whiskey. It went down rougher than expected, but the beer was a welcome relief. He pulled a cigarette from a soft pack of Camels, grabbed a book of matches lying on the counter, and lit it.

The jukebox switched to Duran Duran's "Notorious." On the television, a news reporter blathered on about President Reagan.

Jack noticed his reflection in the mirror behind the bar and saw how intense he looked. He forced a smile, which made him appear mean. For a guy whose luck had changed, he was not taking it in stride. Quite the opposite. He was still waiting for the Lord to punish him.

His mother—God rest her soul—would have told him he was going to hell for what he did. He'd violated one of the Ten Commandments, after all. Although, if he were keeping score, he had broken all of them except, maybe the first. And sometimes, he didn't even believe in the Lord, so he could probably count that one, too.

Perhaps God hadn't seen what he'd just done. His smile relaxed at the thought, and he looked more like his usual self. Could he have gotten away with it because the Lord was too busy to see him do it? Was that so far out of consideration?

"What's so funny?" a woman with dark hair asked.

Jack glanced down the line of patrons to make sure she wasn't talking to someone else.

"You," she said.

The yuppie looked up and smiled.

"Not you, him." She motioned toward Jack. "What's with that goofy grin? You look like the cat who ate the canary, only to find out the bird tasted like shit."

Jack's grin faded. Being remembered for being happy was just as bad as being recognized for being angry.

The brunette slid off her stool and prowled over. She was the same age as him, and her wedding ring let Jack know what kind of woman she was.

"Annette," she said and clicked her drink against his beer can.

"Jack."

Annette leaned close to the yuppie's ear. "Would you mind trading seats?"

The yuppie glanced toward Jack, seemed to consider saying no, but wordlessly abandoned his stool. Dejectedly, he shuffled toward the end of the bar.

Annette sat next to Jack with her body facing him. She had wonderfully bright, green eyes that watched him with curiosity. The moment seemed to stretch out until she caught him eyeing her hand. "Does it bother you?" She wriggled the ring with her thumb.

"Not really."

"Me neither."

The Ten Commandments reentered his thoughts. He'd already violated one of them today. And hadn't he taken the Lord's name in vain? So, two. He'd violated two of them today. What harm was there in breaking the third, especially if he didn't believe in God?

"Enzo," she said, "bring me another."

The bartender nodded and set about making her drink.

Annette leaned in, and Jack smelled a flowery perfume. "Ever been with a married woman?"

"Not today."

She giggled at his joke, maybe a little too forcefully, then lightly touched his hand. Doing so, she noticed the eagle tattoo on his forearm. "Where did you get that?"

"Overseas."

Her eyes filled with excitement. "You were a soldier?"

"Once."

"Ever kill anyone?"

"No," he lied.

"Oh." The exhilaration drained from her eyes. "What did you do in the military?"

"Pretended to care about my country."

When the door to the bar banged open, Annette's hand jumped from his arm. Sunlight washed over the dingy establishment. She turned toward the new arrival and stiffened.

A big man in polyester slacks and a tweed sport coat stalked over. He was several years older than Jack but not yet thirty. His scowl looked practiced, as if he were still trying to perfect it. He dropped a heavy, protective hand on Annette's shoulder. "Who's this, Etta?"

"A guy wanting a friend." Anticipation flared in her eyes. It was the same thing he saw when she asked if he was a soldier.

"A friend?" The big man smirked. "What kind of friend was he looking for?"

"Wait a minute," Jack said. "There's been a mistake."

Using the back of his hand, the big man smacked Jack's shoulder. "Can't you see she's married? She doesn't need friends like you."

Jack tried to stand, but the big man pushed him back onto his stool. Annette squirmed on her seat and her face flushed. Seeing her amusement at the situation annoyed Jack.

"There's been a misunderstanding."

"You calling my wife a liar?"

"Never mind. I'm sorry for the—" he paused to find the right word "—confusion."

Annette leaned toward her husband and whispered into his ear. As she spoke, his face reddened. He abruptly spun toward Jack and decked him, knocking him to the floor.

Jack came up swinging and caught the big man solidly on the chin. Annette squealed with delight and moved away.

The two threw several punches, but neither got the better of the other man. It seemed to be developing into what Jack's father would have called a royal donnybrook until the bartender smacked a baseball bat across Jack's back.

That ended things.

***

"What's your name?" Officer Avery asked. He hadn't introduced himself—the nametag pinned to his shirt did that for him.

Jack remained silent and watched Annette's husband chat with the second officer near the front door. The big man didn't seem worried about how their altercation would be seen through the eyes of the law.

The two bulls arrived soon after the bartender's wallop with the bat. They handcuffed Jack and put him in a booth while they interviewed the various witnesses.

Jack believed that he'd acted appropriately and in self-defense, so things should work out. However, watching

Annette's husband laugh with the other officer concerned him. The big man wasn't handcuffed and now casually smoked a cigarette.

"You can give me your name here," Avery said, "or you can give it to me at booking. Doesn't make a difference to me."

Jack faced the officer. "I'm going to jail?"

"Darn right, you're going to jail. You assaulted an officer of the law."

"He's a—"

"A detective. Newly promoted."

"But I didn't know he was a cop," Jack said. "Besides, he started it."

"Not according to the bartender."

Jack's jaw dropped, and he glanced at Enzo. The old Italian turned sheepishly away.

Officer Avery continued. "He said you got drunk, grabbed Tobias's wife—"

"I wouldn't."

"—and when Detective Wilder told you to knock it off, you slugged him."

"In self-defense."

"That's not the story the witnesses are telling."

Across the room, Detective Tobias Wilder laughed with the other cop.

Jack shook his head. "It doesn't matter what I say, does it?"

"Not really."

"In that case, fuck you."

***

The two uniformed cops dragged Jack into the alley behind the Smuggler's Club. Tobias Wilder led the way. He seemed to have a perk in his step.

"Take me to jail!" Jack hollered. His hands were still cuffed behind his back.

"In time," Avery said. "All in due time."

"What did he do?" the second uniformed officer asked. His name tag read Barrett.

"This mope told me to fuck off."

"He did *what?*"

"Take me to jail," Jack begged.

"Not a chance," Avery said. He tossed Jack onto the alley pavement.

The second officer squatted next to him. "Did you really say that to my partner?"

Jack rolled to his chest. He struggled to pull his knees underneath him, then righted himself. Barrett slugged him in the chin, and Jack collapsed back to the ground.

"I'm still waiting for an answer, scumbag."

"I told you," Wilder said. "This guy's a hard case."

"How about it, Tobias?" Avery asked. "Want to finish what you started?"

The big man stepped forward. "Don't mind if I do."

It was the kick to the head that finally rendered Jack O'Day unconscious.

***

"Where'd you get this?" Avery asked.

Jack leaned over the hood of a police car with his hands still behind his back. Blood ran from his nose and mouth. "Nuh?"

Avery held up the wad of money that he'd pulled from Jack's pocket. "*This*. Where'd you get it?"

"I earned it," Jack mumbled through swollen lips.

"Doing what?"

"I'm a mechanic."

Avery fanned the bills and showed them to Tobias. "No wrench monkey makes this kind of dough. There's gotta be a thousand bucks here."

Tobias leaned into Jack's ear. "Where'd a mook like you get it?"

"I bet he stole it," Officer Barrett said.

"Damn right, he stole it." The detective nodded. "But who'd he steal it from?"

"Your mom," Jack muttered.

Tobias slugged him in his kidney, and Jack squealed.

"What do you wanna bet," Avery said, "that he's one of the guys responsible for the heist at the Wilson Lumber Yard?"

Tobias leaned into Jack. "That true? Were you part of that payroll robbery?"

"Ah, hell," Barrett laughed. "He's pissing himself."

The detective stepped back in disgust. "Do we know where's he staying?"

Avery handed him Jack's room key for the Knight's Inn. "Classy joint."

"Let's go toss the room," Tobias said. "Maybe we can find something interesting."

***

Thirty-two years later, Jack O'Day returned to Spokane, Washington.

He didn't want to come back to the city, let alone the state. The last time he'd been there, he'd been arrested and spent time in Walla Walla State Penitentiary.

However, when a man's only daughter—his only child—is getting married, he doesn't have much choice.

Jack drove six hours from Portland and arrived just before the start of the wedding.

His daughter, Sabina, was in her senior year at Eastern Washington University in Cheney, a small town outside Spokane. She'd met some boy named Nathan Harper that had swept her off her feet. Jack had listened to her talk about the little doofus since her freshman year. He'd graduated the previous semester and now worked at a firm selling stocks.

During the entire drive, Jack hoped Nathan would be more than he imagined.

The church was a beautiful brick building that resembled an English castle. Jack hadn't believed in God since his time in the military, but he still appreciated the architecture.

The wedding march started as Jack walked in. He grabbed an announcement and tried to hide in the back. His ex-wife's new husband, Mitchell, must have been keeping an eye out for him because as soon as he entered, the man stood and waved him to the front. Jack didn't want to call attention to himself, but he couldn't ignore the man either. He lowered his head and hurried forward. He slid into the pew.

"Hiya, Jack," Mitchell whispered.

Jack smiled, and they shook hands. Truth be told, he liked the man. It initially drove Claudia nuts, but she grew to accept it over the years.

Claudia politely kissed Jack on the cheek. "I was getting worried that you wouldn't show."

"I wouldn't miss this for the world."

The groom and his best men were at the front of the church. Nathan Harper looked as Jack had imagined he would on this day. He'd seen pictures of him before, of course, so he wasn't sure why he expected the kid to change suddenly. He was skinny and too pretty for a young man to be. His dark hair was cut and styled in a flamboyant pompadour. Jack was sure the kid never had a hard day in his life.

Everyone in the church stood as Sabina entered. She was beautiful, and those gathered murmured in excitement. Sabina thought "giving away the bride" was an antiquated idea when women were their father's property until married off. Therefore, she wanted to enter and walk the aisle alone. Jack liked her argument and was proud of her decision.

The wedding started on time, and while the preacher talked, Jack glanced across the aisle to check out the groom's side of the family. They seemed an odd-looking bunch, but they probably thought the same of his side of the church.

In the row behind his, near the aisle, was an attractive woman roughly his age. She wore a black dress that complimented her figure. Her skin was alabaster, and it was obvious that she had taken care to protect it. She briefly looked Jack's way, then returned her attention to the front of the church. There was something familiar about her.

He lingered on the woman, hoping she might glance back at him. When she didn't, Jack turned back to watch his daughter pledge her devotion to the doofus.

***

After the wedding, a reception was held at a northside banquet hall.

A DJ played some modern music as everyone walked in. The first song was a whiny number Jack didn't know. Most current music sounded that way to him—irritable and not worth remembering. He made his way to a corner and watched the crowd stake their claim to the tables.

Sabina brought over Nathan, and Jack shook his son-in-law's hand.

"Be good to her." He didn't know what more could be said. He couldn't threaten the kid and embarrass Sabina. Besides, he was never the threatening type.

After a few more words, the young couple took off to introduce each other to more friends and family.

Claudia and Mitchell beamed with pride and stayed close to Nathan's parents. Jack didn't want to interrupt their happiness, so he searched the room for something more entertaining. Very soon, he spotted her at the minibar—the beautiful woman in the black dress. She waited patiently for the bartender to mix a drink.

"They're beautiful kids," Jack said.

She faced him and smiled. "They sure are."

Her bright, green eyes were hard to mistake. It was as if he were looking back through three decades to the woman in the Smuggler's Club.

"How are you related to Sabina?" she asked.

Jack remained silent. While in prison, he imagined a million things he wanted to say to this woman if he were even given a chance. Now, he couldn't think of a single one.

The woman cocked her head, waiting for him to respond.

"I'm Jack," he said finally. "Father of the bride."

"Huh." Her brow furrowed, and she briefly studied him. It was clear the woman didn't remember him. Jack was oddly disappointed. Looking over her shoulder, the woman said, "I thought Mitchell was her father."

"He's her step."

"I didn't know."

"It's okay. Mitch is a good man, and I like him. She probably turned out better with him in her life."

"That's a surprisingly self-aware statement."

Jack shrugged. "I've had a lot of time to think about who I am over the years. So tell me, how are you related to the groom?"

"I'm his aunt." She offered her hand. "Annette Wilder."

As soon as he took her hand, there was a commotion at the front of the room. She glanced beyond Jack, and her smile disappeared. Annette quickly dropped his hand and walked away without a further word.

Jack didn't look back. Instead, he stepped to the bar and ordered a beer.

"Which one?" the bartender asked.

"Doesn't matter."

Jack glanced over his shoulder. Three decades might have gone by, but there stood a man he would never forget. Tobias Wilder seemed bigger than before, especially around the waist. His face carried an angry, permanent scowl. His gray skin looked like scuffed leather left out in the sun for too long. He wore his salt and pepper hair in a flat-top cut.

Tobias hadn't been at the wedding and must have arrived at the reception already drunk. In his right hand, he clutched a beer. He huddled close to Annette, and she flinched as he spoke. People nearby slowly moved away, eyeing the couple as they did so.

Sabina slipped her arm into her father's. "How you doing, pops?"

Jack kissed her on the cheek. "Good."

"I'm glad you're here."

"Me too." He motioned toward Tobias and Annette. "What's the story with those two?"

"Nathan's aunt and uncle?"

"He looks intense."

Sabina glanced around, then whispered, "He's rough on her."

"Meaning?"

"It's the worst kept secret in the family."

"That's a shame."

"He's a retired cop. That's why he's gotten away with it for so long. Hey, I gotta go. There's someone I want to say hello to. I'll come back in a bit."

She touched his hand before hurrying toward a group of young women.

Jack sipped his beer and watched Tobias berate his wife.

***

After the bride and groom left the reception, Jack stepped into the lobby and made a phone call. When he returned, he found Tobias in front of the buffet table. The man swayed with a Budweiser bottle hooked between two fingers.

Sidling up next to him, Jack asked, "What looks good?"

"Nothing," the big man grumbled.

"But it was a nice wedding, huh?"

Tobias grunted but didn't bother looking at him.

Jack glanced around the reception until he located Annette. "Did you get a load of the babe in the black

215

dress?" He jerked a thumb toward Annette as she danced with a little boy in a blue suit.

Tobias stiffened.

Jack leaned over the buffet table to consider the last few shrimp on a serving plate. "You don't see them like her anymore. That's what a woman is supposed to look like. Am I right?"

Tobias set his plate down. "Watch yourself."

"I gotta say, if she has another glass of wine, I'm making a move. Weddings are an aphrodisiac."

The big man frowned and inhaled deeply, expanding his chest like a cobra. Jack pretended not to notice, but he couldn't fail to see how red the man's face was.

Jack eyed Annette. "She looks like the type to throw a leg in a coat closet. Know what I mean?"

Even though Jack knew it was coming, it still hurt like hell. Tobias swung the beer bottle like a man trying to christen a boat, but Jack flinched enough, so the blow glanced more off his shoulder than the side of his head.

He collapsed and protected himself as Tobias attacked. After a couple of kicks into the ribs, the bigger man dropped onto Jack and punched him in the face and chest. Jack absorbed most of the strikes with his arms. He'd gotten to be a decent fighter in prison, yet that was years ago.

Several of the men in attendance tried to intervene, but Tobias yelled at them. "Get back! I'm a cop!" He even swung at one of them. When they backed away, he attacked Jack again.

Two uniformed cops burst into the hall as Tobias punched Jack. For his part, Jack only lay on the floor with his arms covering his head and face. He never hit back.

The older uniformed cop grabbed the big man's shoulder. "That's enough."

Tobias shouted, "I say when it's enough!"

The younger cop, obviously not understanding the danger, reached for Tobias. The angry husband turned and punched the young policeman in the mouth.

"Look what you made me do!" Tobias hollered.

Jack stared up through his arms and prepared himself for another barrage of strikes.

They never came.

Instead, there was a nasty-sounding thump, and Tobias arched his back. He squealed as the older cop struck him a second time with a baton. Tobias collapsed to the floor.

There wasn't much fight then. The two cops handcuffed Tobias—the younger one bleeding from the mouth as they did so—then dragged the big man toward the exit.

Several men helped Jack to his feet. Claudia and Mitchell rushed over and guided him to a nearby folding chair. Claudia bent over and checked his eyes. "Are you okay?"

"I'm fine."

Mitchell asked, "What happened?"

"When you pay a man a compliment about his wife, you don't expect him to hit you with a beer bottle."

"That guy is out of control," Mitchell muttered.

"They should keep him in jail," Claudia said. She turned Jack's face to examine the side.

More cops arrived and separated the witnesses. Jack knew the procedure—they would need to interview them one at a time. He sat patiently. They would get to him soon enough. The music restarted, albeit much softer, and people milled around. Jack could hear the attendees murmuring about the incident. Several came by, patted him on the shoulder, and hoped he was okay.

When the older cop returned, Jack gave him his name and info. The cop jotted it in his notebook. "Mr. Wilder is claiming you said vile things about his wife."

"We were at the buffet table. I'd never met the guy before, and I said some woman looked nice. That was it, and it wasn't vile."

"That woman was his wife."

"So? She still looked nice. I can't help it if the guy can't take a compliment."

The cop scribbled in his notebook and asked a few more clarifying questions until he felt like he had Jack's side of the story. Then he asked, "Did you call nine-one-one?"

"How could I have done that? I was getting my ass kicked."

"A male caller reported a fight here, then hung up. The caller didn't leave his information. Dispatch called back the phone number, but it wasn't answered. The number is associated with this business here."

"As I said, I was getting my asked kicked. You guys saw it."

The cop smirked. "The call came in *before* your fight."

"I don't know what to tell you, except maybe check your clocks. Either way, I lucked out."

"Said the guy who got beat up." The cop handed Jack a business card with a report number written on it. "Are you willing to press charges against Mr. Wilder?"

Jack shrugged. "Can I think about it?"

***

It didn't take much for Jack to get her address. Sabina gave it to him without asking why.

Annette Wilder lived on High Drive with a view of southwest Spokane. Jack rang the doorbell and waited for several moments.

When she opened the door, he could see her as she truly was. Wrinkles were at the edges of her eyes and lips. Time may have marked her, but it didn't make her any less attractive than the first time he saw her.

"I'm sorry," Jack said, although he didn't feel that way.

"For what?"

"For your husband ending up in jail."

"Don't be. It's not the first time he's done this."

"How long will he be in?"

"I'm not bailing him out, so it'll probably be Monday before he's released. He'll take it out on me then. He always does."

"You shouldn't stay here."

"I won't." She cocked her head and studied him. "I know you from somewhere, don't I?"

"From the wedding."

"No, from somewhere else."

Jack nodded. "Thirty years ago, in a bar on Howard Street."

Her eyes went up as she thought. "The Smuggler's Club?"

"Uh-huh."

She covered her mouth. "Oh, my God. That was you?"

"That was me."

Her eyes softened. "I don't know what to say."

"You don't need to say anything."

"No, I do. I should. I was a different person back then."

"We all were."

She frowned now, and sadness crept deeper into her eyes as she remembered. "It is you. I'm so sorry. What happened after they took you outside?"

"I went to prison. Well, jail. Prison came a couple months later."

"For how long?"

"Four years. I got some time off for good behavior."

She covered her mouth again. "I am so sorry."

"Why? You didn't rob the payroll. I did. I was stupid enough to get caught, too. I learned a lot that day in the bar."

Annette glanced around, suddenly aware of a potential danger she might have been in. "Why are you here?" Her voice was small and full of fear.

"I wanted to say something hurtful."

She lowered her gaze. "What is it?"

"It no longer seems worth it."

"You can say it. It's okay. I'm sure I've earned it."

Jack shook his head.

Annette looked up, then pushed the door open. "Would you like to come in? Maybe talk a little?"

"I can't. I'm meeting my ex and her husband for lunch."

"That's very modern of you."

"I'm a modern guy. I grew a little in thirty years."

"You can come by later if you like. Tobias won't be home until tomorrow."

"It's better if I don't."

Annette frowned. "But we never got our chance all those years ago."

"No, we didn't," Jack said.

He turned and left without looking back. He'd said everything he'd wanted to say.

Notes

If you're hanging around to read the notes at the end of a short story collection, you're probably one of those folks who sat through the end credits of *Ferris Bueller's Day Off* only to be rewarded when the title character stuck his head out of a room and asked, "You're still here?"

Ever since then, I've watched movie credits, hoping to find a little slice of joy like that. Of course, Marvel Comic movies have made post-credit scenes seem cliché now, but that moment in 1986 made me realize there might be little pieces of happiness to be found after the cinematic fun and mayhem were over.

So, we've ended up here together. Thank you for reading my tales of crime. I'm hoping you found a story in this collection that you loved. It's okay if you only enjoyed most of them. It's even all right if you disliked one or two.

Major Leaguers can get to the Baseball Hall of Fame by hitting the ball thirty percent of the time. If you hated one of the stories contained herein, then I would consider that striking out at the plate. I took an at-bat, and I whiffed. Or maybe I drove it deep to the wall, but the story's ending curved it foul. At least I got in the box and took a swing.

However, if you liked a third of them, I could earn my way into a short story writer's version of Cooperstown.

If you loved just one of them, then that means I hit it out of the park.

And if you were one of those Ferris Bueller fans, you might remember him sitting in Wrigley Field chanting, "Hey, batter, batter, swing batter."

How about that for tying two disparate thoughts together?

Now, let's talk about some of the stories contained in this collection.

"The Serious Business of Ira Hammerstein," **"Foolproof,"** and **"Death at Sunrise"** were first published in Dark City Book's *Stories for a Dead Night in Spokane*.

I wrote "Ira Hammerstein" in my head while driving out of town one day. It was a two-hour trip in each direction. I didn't listen to the radio and instead started speaking the lines of the story to myself. By the time I returned home, I had the story ultimately worked out. I hurried to my computer and wrote it as I had practiced it over and over. It worked the first time it touched paper.

"Death at Sunrise" has recently been published as a standalone tale in the 509 universe. Its protagonist is Major Crimes Detective Shane McAfee of the Spokane County Sheriff's Office. McAfee returns in the first installment of the Flip-Flop Detective series—*Strait Over Tackle*.

"Foolproof" was my very first reference to the Hope Apartments. I hadn't even conjured up the 509 Crime Stories yet, but I imagined my lead character getting evicted from these apartments as part of his motivation for committing a crime. The Hope makes another appearance in "The Price to Pay." This place of heartbreak and desperation got an anthology treatment as contributing authors took a tour through the world of the 509 in *The Eviction of Hope*.

"Cry Uncle" first appeared in Dark City Book's *Spokane is Still Deader than Dead*. It was one of those stories that grew out of hearing a word or a phrase. Crying uncle means to beg for mercy. However, I saw a child crying out for a favorite uncle to rescue her. The idea of a masked man breaking into a home to save a little girl sprang to mind.

Several previously unpublished stories see their first bit of daylight here.

One of my favorite tales is **"Carter's View."** I loved the idea of a guy up on his roof, getting a unique perspective of his neighborhood. One of the central themes of the 509 Crime Stories is how people and places look differently through the eyes of others. Our own neighborhood can look unusual when we see it from different angles.

"Remember the Rifleman" features an appearance by Jim Morgan, the detective from *The Blind Trust* and *The Value in Our Lies*.

I originally wrote **"Daddy's Girl"** as a standalone tale. The pimp was first named Rolo and ended up in a story set in a world my frequent co-author, Frank Zafiro, created called River City. Even though Frank used Rolo in subsequent tales, I wanted to know what happened to my version of him. So, Rolo was renamed Junior so he could have a life in the 509.

"Dwight's Girl" allowed me to write a bit of a bittersweet tale. Would Marlene, the prostitute, get free and move on with her life? If you've read this far, you know she didn't.

I wasn't done with Marlene, though. After ruining her Christmas and sending her back to Junior, I wanted her to get free. **"Marlene"** allowed me to do just that. Once I had the three interlinked tales together, it felt like they were waiting for something bigger. Marlene and Junior come back to life in *The Mean Street*.

"The Greatest Show on Earth" was meant to be a slice of life tale told through a patrol officer's eyes. I tried to show a bit of the craziness cops see when they respond to a call for service and what they think of while they're on scene.

"Forgive Us Our Sins" was written after a long night of drinking with a friend. I cannot confirm or deny the existence of The Tiptoe Lounge. There is a rumor that such a place exists. I can truthfully say I've never been, although I wish I had been invited.

I wrote **"The Return of Jack O'Day"** years ago, and it had a much different ending then. I was younger (that's how "years ago" works) and immature. It seemed to me that payback had to have some sort of physical nature to it. However, the bittersweet finish—Jack telling Annette that they had indeed missed their chance—was all he needed. It didn't need cruelty. It didn't need one-upmanship. We all live with what-might-have-been moments and the reality that the road we didn't take might have been the one we should be on.

Just like in the first volume, I appreciate you hanging in there and reading to the end. If you loved, liked, or hated any of these stories, I hope you'll send me an email and let me know.

Now, in the parting words of Ferris Bueller, "You're still here? It's over. Go home."

Colin
Spokane, Washington
Summer 2021

About the Author

Colin Conway is the creator of the 509 Crime Stories, a series of novels set in Eastern Washington with revolving lead characters. They are standalone tales and can be read in any order.

He also created the Cozy Up series which pushes the envelope of the cozy genre. Libby Klein, author of the Poppy McAllister series, says *Cozy Up to Death* is "Not your grandma's cozy."

Colin co-authored the Charlie-316 series. The first novel in the series, *Charlie-316*, is a political/crime thriller that has been described as "riveting and compulsively readable," "the real deal," and "the ultimate ride-along."

He served in the U.S. Army and later was an officer of the Spokane Police Department. He has owned a laundromat, invested in a bar, and run a karate school. Besides writing crime fiction, he is a commercial real estate broker.

Colin lives with his beautiful girlfriend, three wonderful children, and a codependent Vizsla that rules their world.